Ruthie

A Life Out of Focus

Gerald Burke Leonard

Hollywood Beach Publishing

Disclaimer

Reference to characters is without identification to any individual, living or dead,.

Chapter 1
I Give You Ruthie Ross

Ruthie wasn't actually her name. . . but she was real by whatever name we call her. And, unfortunately, the turmoil that plagued her very existence was likewise no fairy tale. Ruthie's life was so distended from societal norms that such an existence would have been incomprehensible for most people. For Ruthie, however, one nightmare after another simply defined her sad existence – a set of conditions she was handed at birth.

If one believes in omens and symbolism, Ruthie had been born under an ominously dark cloud, both literally and figuratively. A sudden shift in the jet stream had turned the normal chill of the seasonal rain to sleet which slashed against the windows of the hospital's maternity ward in a nearly horizontal plane. The half-frozen icy bits tinkled against the window pane and added to the distraction as the wind howled with a special ferocity known as a Canadian Downdraft – winds driven from the Arctic across the barren lands of Canada into the upper Midwest. Tomorrow's forecast foretold a deluge of snow. Tonight, however, would be filled with driving winds and a stinging blanket of sleet which combined would result in a daunting treachery of black ice on the roads – that unseen nightmare that terrified drivers. Mr. Ross, however, had been initiated previously through some thirty odd years of growing up in the Midwest, first in Ypsilanti, Michigan, until a downturn in the auto industry "drove" him away and now in Muncie, Indiana, where he had become a tool and die maker for an auto parts manufacturer.

On this night, Mark Ross braved the physical affront that Mother Nature threw his way. After, jumping the battery in his spiffy two-tone DeSoto, he made his way across town to the university hospital, great trepidation being his driving companion. That night, he thought upon subsequent reflection, had been as miserable as those he had spent crammed in an earthen hole just inside the perimeter of the forest that surrounded Bastogne in Belgium where he and his 101st Airborne Division buddies had endured the Battle of the Bulge. Mark Ross would endure these hardships to be with his wife who had been taken to the hospital unexpectedly while he was on his night shift at the plant. They wanted this child she would bring forth on this miserable night; the child would dissolve any thoughts about weather, pain or suffering. They wanted this child; really wanted this child . . . . as they had wanted the previous three lost to miscarriages.

There had not been time for a family before Mark's call up to service for World War II and his wounds had made the process difficult physically following his return.   Now the Ross's were having the child they desperately wanted.

The antiseptic walls of the maternity ward glistened in the harsh light of the delivery room where a team of doctors struggled with what should have been a routine delivery. Gladys Ross had been told by her attending physician, Clarence Morton, that she looked fine and to expect no complications. That was before the delivery had begun and the oversized head of the baby become something of a square peg in a round hole, so to speak.

As the doctor's attempts to stem the flow of blood that hemorrhaged from Gladys Ross's womb demonstrated, Morton's incapacity to navigate through what had become a difficult procedure, an urgent call was sent out through the hospital for assistance in the delivery.

One might think that Dr. Morton was being altruistic in his concern for his patient, wanting nothing more than to deliver a healthy baby and provide for the comfort and health of the mother. It had crossed Morton's mind that his prognosis provided to the patient in writing and the trauma through which she was currently stressing could well be grounds for a malpractice suit. With his back to the wall, he did the most prudent thing he could think of: *cover his ass. . . at all costs.* Find a way to share the problem and deflect responsibility.

Fortunately for Morton, and more importantly for Mrs. Ross, there was a bright young woman finishing her residency at the hospital and concluding her coffee break when the panic of the delivery room hit a crescendo. It was the skills of the young resident that brought the nightmare to an acceptable conclusion and the baby was finally delivered. Not only had she brought the difficult delivery to a successful conclusion, she saved the mother's life and the doctor's career. These facts would be lost in the doctor's report to the hospital administration. The resident had *merely assisted* due to the complications and the need for an additional pair of hands.

A healthy child had been born but not without overshadowing problems.. Rounded shoulders, chunky legs and arms and a head that had only passed through the cervix with great difficulty made Ruthie the largest delivery in the hospital for quite some time. Her large head had been the most difficult aspect of the delivery. The pushing of the large cranium through the small opening nearly tore the mother apart and had the effect of elongating the baby's head, rather dramatically. The pleasant resident physician assured the mother than the baby would be fine and that the head would reshape itself to normal dimensions over the next few months.

The nightmare had unfolded while Mark Ross raced across town through the violent weather. He wanted to be present to help his wife and reassure her through the process, however, by the time Mark arrived at the hospital Ruthie had been born, a little pink bow had been taped to the crown of her head in the absence of enough hair to hold the bow.

In fact, by the time Mark arrived at the hospital, he was greeted by a robust, wailing daughter as pink as cotton candy and as loud as a rock band. Truly a healthy child had been born but not without complications. The birthing process had torn Gladys Ross asunder. So much damage was done, in fact, that Gladys nearly bled to death before the doctors were able to stem the flow and stabilize her condition. For Ruthie's part in the delivery, the tight opening and the large head worked in just the opposite manner.

Gladys Ross dozed into an induced stupor to allow the drugs to initiate the healing process. Mr. Ross sat through the night holding her hand – he held it in love, in concern for her health, and in happiness that they had finally succeeded after three abortive attempts in preceding years. It was mid-morning when Mr. Ross was coaxed awake by a nurse wanting to tend to his wife. She ushered him toward the nursery with directions for the cafeteria where he could shake the chill with some hot coffee before bracing once again for a bout with the weather.

The following day, the proud and jubilant parents accepted the doctors' words of comfort, wrapped their bundle of joy into some cozy blankets after the customary two-day stay following delivery and ventured into the wilds of central Indiana weather. As on the day of delivery, Mark found the driving tedious as he slipped and slid his way toward home over the icy streets, his wipers banging out a rhythmic pattern of sound as they failingly tried to move the crusting ice and snow that was accumulating.

The city's major hospital was on the opposite side of town from the Ross's modest, clapboard house. They had to travel past the university complex, through the downtown area of Muncie and then turn north along Route 67 before turning back to the east to get to their part of town, literally on the other side of the tracks. Enough traffic had sloshed its way along these major arteries to dissipate the buildup of snow somewhat but patches of ice still lay beneath the frothy accumulation on the surface.

As Mark pushed forward along Route 67, the major north-south access road into town, traffic had thinned out and there were those, predictably, who opted to push the laws of nature and the common sense approach to driving under these conditions. Mark Ross was not one of these individuals, at least not today with his new daughter in the car. Three blocks from his turn off to the east side, a large gravel truck barreled down the intersecting street in an attempt to catch the green light – he didn't. The light had changed but his momentum was propelling him forward along with the fear of trying to stop under these hazardous conditions. It would be a gamble the driver had concluded was worth the risk, after all, his was a multi-ton truck loaded with large crushed stone. . . he'd be okay.

The crash occurred predictably at perilous speed. The Ross's car was traveling unabated through a green light in a mild rush to get home to get the baby snug into its awaiting crib. The massive gravel truck traveling beyond the speed limit, beyond common sense, through a red light smashed headlong into the passenger door of the unsuspecting Ross's. The truck driver had "T-boned" them at high speed through limited visibility and had never seen the event taking shape. The impact was loud, a terrifying sound even to bystanders and those busy in the warmth of their nearby homes. The thunderous impact preceded the sound of sheet metal being ripped and shredded.

The speed of the truck sent the Ross vehicle rolling side-over-side landing upside down and barely recognize-able as a passenger car – it might have been some spooky carnival ride at the fairgrounds but not a passenger car.

Moments passed. The only sound now was he whistle of the wind whipping across the torn metal. Then a siren. Distant. . . but drawing nearer. Mr. Ross was dazed with a gash across his forehead and blood streaming down across his blurred vision. No sound from Gladys Ross. Ruthie was clearly present as her trumpeting sound signaled the need for immediate salvation.

When the fire department and ambulance personnel arrived at the scene they found a large gravel truck sitting belligerently in the middle of the intersection. Other vehicles, driven by petulant individuals, wove in-and-out through the turmoil to avoid having to commit to assist or to impede their personal schedule. Then the rescue personnel found the Ross vehicle, upside down in the front yard of the property on the opposite side of the intersection. It had not started to burn but it was clear they would find terrifying consequences when they began to pry open the vehicle.

All three passengers in the car were crumpled up like rag dolls in the upturned vehicle. Mr. Ross was the first extracted from the driver's door. His head was cut with a deep gash running east to west across his brow but it would not be life-threatening. In pulling him out rather unceremoniously to get to

7

the more seriously injured passengers the rescuers concluded one broken leg and one arm with multiple fractures also existed.

There was a tiny infant, they discovered. It was covered in blood. Was it the baby's or was it the mother's? They couldn't be certain at this juncture. One of the medical personnel began the process of tenderly cleaning the baby and decided that there were some abrasions and contusions suffered by the infant, however, the vast majority of the blood had to be the mother's.

A slender fireman scraped his arms bloody as he crawled into the smoldering vehicle and measured for the pulse of the mother. He probed her wrist for a pulse but found none; then he discovered the arm had been severed from her body. He gasped at the sight and the realization of his error. He tried the jugular vein and pressed to detect some sort of rhythmic response. Despite his own pain he lingered in the painfully awkward posture with a prayer on his lips that the pulse was just irregular due to the body trauma. He waited and pressed till his fingers turned white. Tears slid down his cheeks as he finally conceded. . . there was no pulse.

There was also no way by which to extract the mother from the vehicle, not at this time and not under these conditions. Her body had become intermingled with the twisted and torn metal of the door that had been crumpled around her. It would be another full day before she could be separated from the metal and then there would be no chance for an open casket funeral –

not enough of her could be withdrawn in one piece to make that possible.

When Gladys was laid to rest, Ruthie was one week old. At one week of age Ruthie was a motherless child and her father, Mark Ross, began to drink with an abandon that would have overshadowed a sailor. The newborn child had become a casualty as well as the mother who had died a horrific death and even worse, a casualty due to the father's need for rot gut whiskey.

Ruthie's infant years languished from the absence of love and no parental care. Only the neighbor ladies who stole into the house during Mr. Ross's drunken binges saved Ruthie from a certain death. The baby's misshapen head, the body trauma and the physical and psychological damage of the collision represented a mounting set of issues for Ruthie that seemed to grow with each passing month and each passing year. Ruthie as a baby eventually yielded to her becoming a young child and in turn morphed into adolescence in spite of the adversities and without regard to Ruthie's inabilities to function at a peer level. One man in one instant had doomed Ruthie to a lifetime of rejection and suffering, physically, socially and intellectually. Fortunately, she remembered nothing of the event and no one had ever explained the tragedy to her.

In spite of the odds, in spite of the circumstances of her care, Ruthie grew to the age for junior high school. She was not prepared scholastically but the neighbor ladies had intervened with the Department of Child Services to attempt an entry into

9

the world outside the four walls that had been a sort of prison. The "do-gooders" felt that getting into the world along with children her age would permit the maturational process to catch her up. But just how traumatized had her head injuries been? No one had actually measured her intellectual or emotional capacities. What was she about to face? Ruthie certainly had no idea.

Chapter 2
A Young Girl Dreams

Despair is no one's friend. Yet hope can be as distant as the furthest star. And when life has dealt you a hand without so much as a pair, you must make the best of the high card. . . and bluff – bluff the hell out of the others when that is all you have. At the end of the day, whether the bluff worked or not, one still has one's own conscience with which to deal. One must a find a balance between lost opportunities and the promise of tomorrow, between the taunts and ridicule and the belief that these are only a cover up for the other person's own insecurities. The secure individual is one who knows what is in his or her heart and how that can manifest itself to the outside world.

Dreams lie somewhere between hope and despair, between make-believe and reality, and between you and those people and events that torment your soul. They are the stuff from which one's imagination can propel itself beyond the tethered practicalities of the daytime conundrum of work, schedules, confusion, fear, hate, and loathing. Sleep brings to the front door the possibility of undiluted greatness and all the wonders achieved by others – they are now at your own doorstep, only a few blinks away as one dreams his or herself into another world.

Dreams cannot be confused with nightmares. They are not the flipside of the same coin. Nightmares are the inescapable infliction by the devil to never let one's conscience find solace and peace in the escape from the day's reality. Nightmares are much like a dentist's tool that pokes and scratches, digs and wiggles its way into the tiniest crevices of a tooth to the *dark side* with hideous pain and suffering. Nightmares are the dark side's way of never releasing the soul from torment and anguish.

Ruthie's mother who had been torn apart by the shredding metal of the collision that crumpled the car into a knotted, twisted mess is a reminder how ugly life can be without reason or explanation. A father who refuses to accept responsibility for the child left behind, a child with a clinical assessment of some degree of brain damage resulting from the birthing process brings an ever present reminder forth that life is cruel; it is not for the weak. Images of the drunken slurs, the back-hands, the ever present whores, the absence from the house when there is no food, no heat, no money are images wrought by the dark side. They don't fade as one tries to curl into the fetal position to find that warm place long ago vacated. They stand at the front of the mind and bang on the head of the bearer. They twist pictures and thoughts around like a tornadic storm. Up becomes down; left becomes right; the back becomes the front. The mind whirls and loses focus in its attempt to run from these assaults on the subconscious – but still they don't stand down.

Only a pure heart can see through this cloud. The cloud is dark and ominous; it threatens at every moment by sending bolts of lightning through the cranial cavity, so many electrical impulses wherein the neurons continue to fire their charge throughout the mind even when the bearer thinks it is shut down. A select few, the chosen ones, can obviate the debilitating effects of the dark side. It is these chosen few who can slide between the visual assaults on the mind and the incredulous pain that follows and find hope beyond. They are the saints, the young children. They are those whose reasoning power has been damaged through some infliction. . . a car accident.

As a young girl Ruthie clawed her way through the day. Most children are possessed in an envelope of love and nurturing. Ruthie had been abandoned. . . first by a mother whose untimely death left the infant with one parent – one who no longer wanted her as she reminded him of the loss he had suffered. Mark Ross proved to be a man who needed his cup to overflow before considering the needs of others, namely, Ruthie. As time wore on, this condition proved only to worsen. The dimensions of his disconsolate demeanor spun into a full blown picture of denial and lack of concern. He had his drink; he had his ever-present whore. The screaming child locked in another room, well, she just screamed. Others saw to her irregular feeding and changing of soiled clothes. Rather than bolt he remained in this self-made hell hole because the insurance settlement had been predicated upon the benefit being for Ruthie's care – he had to appear to go through the motions and abandoning her (formally) wouldn't work.

The child cried, screamed, wet herself, ate paint chips from the deteriorating walls. She let her eyes follow the wandering rats that found slim pickings in her room. They shared the same food scraps, eating alternately without thought on the part of either of dangers. The ten-by-ten room became Ruthie's world for nearly eight years much like that of a prisoner. Her shackles were her father's rage and the fear that bound her tightly, in a psychologically and socially knotted ball of fear.

In spite of the occasional beatings to stop the crying, in spite of the malnutrition, in spite of the veritable captivity within her home Ruthie did survive. Her body was still there, undernourished as it was but her mind was not. That contradiction seems to be what saved Ruthie. The slow, agonizing extraction with forceps from her mother's womb had damaged her brain - this diminished capacity is what probably gave Ruthie a chance at life even though many would say that the brain damage represented a life already lost.

Ruthie recognized rage. She heard the tumult and hatred in her father's voice. She could see the rage in his eyes even when they were totally out of focus due to inebriation. What she couldn't do, however, was to analyze what she saw and heard. The shouting was so continual, the abuse a constant and the complete disregard was a perpetual condition. It was all she knew. These things scared her but she had not the capacity to evaluate the meaning of what she was seeing and hearing. She had no frame of reference. She was alone. There were no siblings. There were no friends and neighbor children had been strictly warned to leave well enough alone. Her sense of balance depended on the degree of severity, how long it was between meals, the frequency of being offered the chance to change into clean, unsoiled clothing. Her wants were, therefore, very simple and without the frame of reference she had no concept of just how miserable her life was – it was what it was. For what she knew, everyone's life was probably the same.

The brain damage had been God's blessing to protect the child and give her a chance to get to maturity where there would be at least a minimal chance to survive.

God gave Ruthie another break when she was a year or so away from the age to attend junior high school. Her father died.

The police saw the death a little different. Their conclusions were based on the facts that Mark Ross had been found lying in a pool of vomit and blood, his pants at half-mast and his manhood cut away in a rather crude manner. The joke around the force had become the question as to which of the whores had finally taken enough of his shit.

In the process of their investigation, they discovered a locked room. . . and a young girl.

Life in the large institutional building would prove to not be the harangue that "home" had been. At least for her simple mind there seemed to be a noticeable improvement. The ladies in the hooded black uniforms with white, starched frames around their smiling faces were nice. They didn't scream, they didn't beat her. . . there were no rats to watch, no paint chips to eat. The electrical torment that had since birth danced about in her head causing blinding pain behind her eyes seemed to fade away. It was replaced by images of brightness rather than darkness. There were images of various people, young, old, some with canes, some dressed nicely, some in a hurry, tall, short and many children. There were now images of things that made her smile, made her look forward to her naps and the nights. No more skittering of clawed feet about the window sill. Instead the images were of dolls, of food, of the faces of other children and of people young and old – smiling.

Chapter 3
Developing Values

Values, like leaves, don't grow on trees – not in the winter time, not in Muncie, Indiana.

Ruthie had lost what little frame of reference she had when her father died, unexpectedly, she thought – predictably as many observers had thought . . .hoped for.

The nuns at St. Jerome's orphanage had picked up the shards of humanity that they found locked in the bedroom in the rear of the crumbling house on the eastside. They began a process to imbue a spirit of hope in the girl – at least that was their goal and their belief they were achieving God's work.

It was a bit of a setback for the elderly women ensconced in their black-and-white habits when Ruthie finally mouthed her first words for them: "shit, piss, fuck, bastard, hate, shit, fuck you."

Ruthie left her indelible and unique mark on the cloistered halls of St. Jerome's from her first words forward. The nuns reverberated as if jolted by sticking a fork into an electric outlet. They knew the words, they had never used them or even heard them. All their sensibilities were lightning-struck and the fear of God's wrath falling upon their small convent descended upon them as if Lucifer himself had stepped from the virulence of the young girl's frothing mouth – her eyes wildly seeking focus as her body flailed about as if possessed.

Ruthie was eight years old. The nuns had a call to make: they could discard her like so much human rubbish or they could persevere and attempt to redeem her soul and find a way to establish a human presence in the girl who had known no such values. A vote was cast and despite their vows and the directives from the mother house, the vote was almost unanimous to send the girl off to the county facilities as a ward. In the county facility there would be no treatment. There were Spartan meals; there were walls, high walls and a locked gate. There were no programs. There was no hope.

St. Jerome's pastor prevailed upon his nuns. The cherubic Irishman from Cork reminded the sisters of their vows made to God and to the parish. And while he wouldn't force them to reconsider their position, he did manage to eke out a healthy dose of guilt associated with their selfish vote and that any inherent fear they might have as to the care and instruction of this lost soul, she was nonetheless a *child of god*.

The Old Testament taught Jews fear while the Catholics learned guilt. The rebuke to the nuns was like a father's review of a child's substandard report card. The hooded ladies had to accept the chastisement and move forward even though their individual feelings were less a commitment than their collective vows.

Lathered in a bath of guilt the nuns caved in to the manifest guilt and the realization that the priest was right. It was their job and it was their calling. To walk away from Ruthie would have been an act of perversity so profound by the standards to which they subscribed that they had no choice but to swallow the degrading verbal blasts from the demon child and get on with process of healing – giving Ruthie a benchmark set of values with which to modify her impure life.

As time passed, Ruthie slowly became a respectable, if not respectful, prodigy of the nuns' value system. The metamorphosis was being delivered by a group of *old women* who had not known fornication, drink, vile language or the kind of depravity in which they found Ruthie. The nuns prayed for guidance to look into the mind of an eight year old girl and find a common ground whereupon they could build another redeemable soul for the Lord.

What is it they say about a silk purse and a sow's ear. . .? Ruthie was the quintessential example – the "powers that be" were trying to conform the diminished-capacity, "shut-in" young girl into the stereotype for girls of her age. The saying notwithstanding, the nuns were stalemated in their attempt to bring the young girl to a state of conformity.

It couldn't realistically be determined whether or not Ruthie had ever tried, whether she was just uncommonly stubborn, or if she had a neurologic problem so deeply rooted in her psyche that it would take clinicians, not nuns, to expunge the demonic behavior exhibited by the young girl. Following the priest's admonishment, the ladies in black rededicated themselves to not giving up. In weighing in on their lack of success, there was the clear realization of apparent brain damage, as well as the environmental considerations wrought by living in the same house with an alcoholic, whore-mongering sadist. The question: did this extent of damage have irreversible impacts?

Blanchard Avenue was the kind of street that children did not cross unattended. Four lanes of fast-moving traffic with drivers who seldom conceded to conventionality or legal requirements made crossing the street a challenge, at the least. Ruthie had no reason to cross the street, but she sat on the curb whiling away her time with no apparent thought in her mind. Just the sound of the cars whizzing by seemed pacify the child's feeble mind. Abruptly, this changed with the shrieking of tires, cursing from down-rolled windows, and the clash of metal against metal as a small puppy wound its way across the hundred foot wide chasm of death. The puppy knew no more about the hazards associated with Blanchard Avenue than did Ruthie but they both dealt with its realities in a mindless manner. The car-honking ceased, a small fuzzy puppy emerged from just in front of a large pickup truck's tire and avoided certain death by no more than an inch.

"C'mere boy. C'mere. Yeah, Ruthie will play with you." The wooly little ball of a mongrel puppy was seduced away from the wiles of breakneck traffic onto the curb where Ruthie sat staring into oblivion, wondering about life, albeit without the sophistication of meaningful knowledge, theories, or abstract logic. She wondered if the nice ladies in the black-and-white outfits would feed her again today. She wondered if the pain in the back of her head would persist again today driving her to tears as with almost every day. She wondered if the little puppy would be squashed by a speeding car.

"C'mere boy. . . that's it. Yeah, come to Ruthie." With that Ruthie evidenced her first spoken language beyond the string of expletives she could chain together which seemed to carry an harmonic cadence, much like she had heard continually since her mother had died. After all, language was a learned development, an environmentally-founded copy picked up from those around the developing child.

The ball of fuzz, dappled in discordant colors bounced over the curb and ran into the area between Ruthie's spread legs. She stroked across the back of his little head as he sprung his front legs up into her lap, his tongue wagging – a dog's smile, a picture of happiness – he'd found someone to care. So had Ruthie. "Little fella, you're going to be my special friend. I'll give you part of my meals and you can stay with me. Okay?" Three quick *yipes* seemed to respond affirmatively.

Ruthie smiled and laid back into the grass, her sneakered feet extending off the curb. The little puppy waddled its way unevenly over her torso until he was within licking distance. He licked her chin, he licked her cheeks, he licked her nose and her lips and Ruthie was ecstatic. She had a friend, a true friend. This friend would not swear or lock her into a room. This little friend would defend her from the pesky rats if the orphanage had any. She would keep him in a box in her room. She was lucky, she now understood. She had troubled over the fact that every other girl in the ward slept side by side on steel cots arranged in two long rows, one on either side of the room. Only Ruthie had a private room and this had initially caused her great consternation. It was a solitary confinement once again. She had thought that she was being isolated as punishment. The reality, never shared with her, was the fact that the nuns feared for the other girls should Ruthie rise into one of her rages. There was no way of telling what Ruthie might do and without professional care and observation there was no clinical assessment as to the conditions that governed her behavior, just the behavior of the old women who had never before experienced such ungodly acts or language.

Now, Ruthie discovered a whole new meaning to the term isolation. It was the way by which she would be able to keep the little doggie without the interference of the other girls vying for its attention or the demanding conditions by the nuns to *get rid of that thing*.

Ruthie would be able, now, to share the small room with her friend without the prying eyes of the others, play with the little guy, and develop a friendship that she had never known.

"You need a name, little fella. What should I call you?" She pondered the dilemma being the only real test of her ability to cognitively make any form of judgment up to this point in her life. "You're Bob. Of course, you're Bob." The two were almost nose to nose as she talked to the animal, she all smiles and he, his tail wagging at a furious rate throughout. The two made their way back into the ward at the orphanage. Some of the other girls had looked curiously at the peculiar protrusion under Ruthie's cardigan as the lump continued to twist and squirm about as if she truly was possessed by some kind of demonic presence as had been rumored.

Once in her room she set about setting up a little home for Bob and found some of her uneaten lunch that she fervently fed to the little beggar. When she was done she continued to stroke the mangy coat worn by the street dog. He would need a bath but that would be a problem if she were to avoid discovery but she'd find a way. She made that judgment.

It took a couple days, but the nuns discovered Bob had taken up residence with Ruthie. Consternation was all some of the older nuns could manage. Hissy-fit might be a term to best fit the behavior of the older ladies in black-and-white. The mother superior's attitude was less gracious, it nearly paralleled that to which Ruthie had been witness for nearly eight years. It terrified her much as her father had done to which she responded by crawling into a boxed-in corner and crying hysterically. The language returned and the nuns ran from the room crossing themselves in that gesture that Catholics use to emulate the crucifixion of Christ on the cross. But then a small miracle happened as the mother superior's last vindictive threat sailed through the air like a lead balloon to slam into the already damaged mind of the young girl – Bob crawled into Ruthie's lap and began to lick at her chin and then her cheek. The child can't be hysterical when a cuddly, little puppy begins licking her face and wagging his tail as if to say, *"hey, friend, I'm here for you. You don't have to cry. Please stop. Please. Hey, I want some more food, ya got any?"*

Before she had the door fully closed, the mother superior saw what happened. She saw the uncontrollable eight year old child, who swore like a drunken whore mongering sadist and who demonstrated qualities that she thought may require an exorcism melt away before her eyes. The puppy had soothed the savage beast and brought a level of docility to the troubled child that none of the sisterhood had been able to achieve. Mother Superior Margaret Mary Sorenson crossed herself about six times in rapid succession, and perhaps even smiled as she quietly closed the door. It had been a miracle. At the least it had been a sign. The nun's entire outlook on life was molded around a belief system that the Lord is God, that he is good and will take care of those who need his help. She had just seen it. He had delivered the puppy to the one person not reachable by any normal channel. She trumpeted a comment to the other girls as she strode down the aisle toward the outer door, "you leave that child alone and leave her puppy alone. Anyone bothering her or messing with that little dog will have me to answer to. Understood?" A group of nearly twenty girls stood dumbfounded, mouths agape as they grappled to understand the edict just handed to them by the goose-stepping six foot, four inch Mother Superior as she broke through the door into the blinding sunlight. The nun couldn't move her long limbs fast enough to the rectory to share the experience with the pastor. "Father! Father!.... "

Bob and Ruthie matured together – Bob into a truly ugly dog and Ruthie into a reasonable semblance of a pre-teen girl, but one whose reasoning capabilities were impaired nonetheless. Poor Bob did not age well. If ever there were a poster for dog-neutering, Bob would have been given the starring role. His coat was not a silky sheen; it was more a mottled imbalance of colors, shaggy here and matted there. At the same time, Ruthie had moved from her tender age of eight up to twelve under the un-likely balance of care-giving from the nuns and from Bob. Bob on the other hand couldn't claim person-years in his maturation process. He had slid from a month old to middle-age, but the need or ability to worry about such trivia was not within Bob's genetic makeup. He was happy – he had Ruthie, nothing else mattered to Bob. The two were inseparable, even at the manda-tory attendance at mass once each week. Ruthie was permitted to sit in the rear pews with Bob anchoring the pew on the terraz-zo tiles.

Shortly, Ruthie's agenda would change. The administra-tors of the orphanage had been conditioning the child for nearly two years to build a strong case for the reality of change when it finally occurred. The junior high school was quite a distance away and in a short time she would be that age and have to at-tend. She would be moving on with her life at the ripe old age of twelve and experiencing her own form of post-partum anxiety.

Formally, the process called for Ruthie to become a ward of the state and be put into a foster home as her social and communicative skills had blended enough into a socially-acceptable form to suggest her ability to function within the broader context of society. Thank you, Bob.

Chapter 4
Junior High School

The number of adjustments from the cloistered world of the orphanage and convent to the "real world" was devastating – the extent of change would be a challenge to any student. For Ruthie, it would be terrifying. It was, after all, the real world and the only static condition in the real world is that change for adolescents is a natural evolutionary process.

Ruthie had only known two rooms in her twelve years of life – the first, a veritable prison and the second, a cloistered sanctum sanctorum, or in English, a prison. Now, however, there was a third and it would take some getting used to as well. Everything was effectively out of place: the dresser was here instead of there. The closet was on the far wall, not the near. The window slid to the side instead of lifting from the bottom. *Downers. Downers. Downers.* However, a bright light, she reasoned. The room had its own adjoining bathroom. *Definitely a positive.* No more gliding past a host of peering eyes as you hold your privates on the dash to the porcelain. This was a luxury. The other chit for peace of mind was that the Radcliffe's had agreed to let Ruthie keep the dog in her room, providing of

27

course she took complete responsibility for its upkeep and feeding. To Ruthie's way of thinking, no other course of action would have been half way logical. Of course, she would walk the dog, clean up after it, feed it, and above all – love it.

There was more now to Ruthie's world than just the singular room. She was expected to eat at the breakfast and dinner tables with her state-appointed guardians, or pseudo-parents. She was expected to interact with their ten year old daughter. She was having to pay attention to what was said to her and try to grasp the rules of society as Mr. Radcliffe explained them to her – smile, be polite and friendly, never say anything mean or use bad language. He was asking a lot, especially in the last category. Ruthie had not forgotten the leverage she felt, the absolute power that seemed to emanate from her use of the concatenated string of expletives: *shit, piss, fuck, bastard, hate, shit, fuck you.* There had to be something magical in those words she had long since concluded. They seemed to possess a great deal of sway with adults and for other kids her age, they would often run away in tears. Those words had to mean something powerful. She'd set those aside for now, though, and tried her best to please Mr. and Mrs. Radcliffe. They treated her nicely, gave her a doll, some other silly toys, warm meals and smiles. She could almost feel Bob licking her cheek when the Radcliffe's sat face-to-face with her and spoke softly about what a nice girl they thought she was and about the progress she was making at adapting to the new environment. But there were demons with which to deal nonetheless.

Ruthie's comfort level with her new environment grew progressively in the months that preceded her next intervention – junior high school. Her adaptation was manifest in her growth spurt. She was gaining weight. . . prodigiously. It might have been the comfort of the environment. It might have been the quality of the food, or the regularity of the meals. It might have been genetics. Regardless, Ruthie's physical development blossomed pushing her beyond the norms for a twelve year old girl, past the norms for an adolescent, all the way to the veritable middle-age spread and in to a new crisis. If her life wasn't one crisis, it was another.

Junior high school is a make-it or break-it time in the emotional development of a young person. Ruthie approached the school's steps and the curiosity of junior high school with great trepidation. Her schooling had been ad hoc at best by the nuns and them some home-schooling by the Radcliffe's to provide a threshold for justifying her schooling. While the Radcliffe's and Ruthie were focused on the minimal academics to sustain her through the challenges that lay ahead they had overlooked the obvious – the social pressures associated with her physical endowment.

The young woman leaped past her pre-teen peers to an astonishing 38 triple D in the upper torso region – a number that the young boys could get their minds around but never their grimy little hands. That was a blessing, even if a mixed blessing. The downside was the fact that her waist had mushroomed to an unhealthy forty-eight inches, her thighs looked like the trunks of flourishing redwoods and she had hips that precluded entry through many a doorway. To keep her emotional stability in balance, she felt her breasts – *the boys called them boobs* - were still blossoming. Ruthie realized her ungainly weight was a problem but hoped that the boys would focus on her chest and not be repelled by her other shortcomings that seemed to literally and figuratively weigh her down.

Junior high school might be considered the developmental pinnacle. Life to this point had been an adroit level of preparation for the smack in the jaw that adolescence and junior high promise. This unfortunate condition is a turning point upon which one's future is so often cast and based largely on the cards that are dealt and how they are played.

Muncie CJHS, the junior high, had quite a reputation: the building was solidly built from brick and Indiana limestone. Its reputation, unfortunately, didn't extend into the realm of academics or inter-social development. In short, it completely lacked what Ruthie so desperately needed. Teens, and Ruthie in particular, needed it to be more than just a haven from the cold weather. Sadly, it wasn't.

Ruthie wandered through her three year requirement to CJHS most likely without ever embracing a smile. But then, what was there to smile about. . . she had become the butt of jokes throughout the school. Even as a ninth grader, the seventh graders ribbed her to her face with "fatty, fatty, two by four, couldn't get through the bathroom door. . . so what'd she do but

30

go on the floor." The jokes cut to the core. The stares and pointing bruised her already ruptured ego. Her clothing and attempt at makeup simply exacerbated her conundrum. She was caught. She was required by state law to remain in school until she turned sixteen. The State of Indiana had in a de facto sense decreed that Ruthie Ross had to show up daily and take the jibes, the pokes, the sneers and the jeers. She was a laughing stock, a reality that even many of the teachers were loath to bypass with their sharp, little and pointless barbs.

As with all students at this age and through this rite of passage, Ruthie was required to take the fundamental building block courses to prepare her for high school – a reality that Ruthie could barely face – there were many more students at MCHS, the high school and she knew what that would mean.

Ruthie's courses included the compulsory English lessons, Mathematics, World History, the History of Indiana, a general science course and a few other meaningless attempts to keep the kids off the streets until three in the afternoon. Ruthie's favorite class had quickly evolved to be her math courses. The teachers had prejudged her lack of skill and interest and simply bypassed her involvement in the class. She was permitted to sit for the prescribed hour long assault on her intellectual potential while she doodled on the edges of blank homework papers. Her least favorite subjects. . . English, World History, the History of Indiana, Science and anything else. One awkward after another seemed to propel her into having to try to respond to a challenge by the teacher to either answer a question, explain why she did not turn in her homework, or to simply stay awake. . . when sleep was such a forgiving blessing.

Sleep. Whether at home after school, tucked away at night, or during the laborious discussions about some character in a play in her English class, sleep was a blessed event. This was the one forgiving opportunity to escape and be someone, someone special, someone she could admire and the others would emulate. At night her sleep was often interrupted by gun fire from somewhere within the neighborhood or by a ranting, drunken father on one of his intermittent stays at home or it might even be a scream from the other bedroom in their dreary house where a five dollar hooker was being beaten as part of her father's interpretation of intercourse. Trying to sleep had become more of a challenge at night than a respite and it usually came only after she had popped a pill. Ruthie neither understood nor did she care about the long term impacts upon the health of her body. It was sufficient that the little yellow pills allowed her to slide into a state of delirium in which her single-minded fantasies took control and the nightmares of the day were shunted to some recess of her mind. This was the one opportunity to avoid conflict, distasteful comments, the taunting and stares and the overwhelming feelings of inadequacy. The pills were cheap and easily obtained. Many others were digging for ten dollars, twenty-five dollars or even fifty dollars in some cases to find a chemical outlet for their woes but Ruthie had only to jerk down the top of her ill-fitting dress or rip away at the buttons to display her amplitude to the awaiting eyes and hands of Manny "the dealer" to get a pill for the night. She was not offended by the need to pull her bosom out for display even if others saw the event. They were, after all, her proudest possession – actually possessions – and she knew that given the opportunity to have the proper venue to showcase her "talent" she would win the hearts and minds of all the boys and men and drive the other girls insanely jealous. She just needed an opportunity and junior high school had not proved to be that venue. There were too many *buzzards* sitting on the telephone poles staring down at her every move, too many critics about every syllable that she uttered, too many bureaucrats to decry the quality of her appearance, her clothing, her wretched home and life therein. The entire social fabric into which she had been cast represented a paralyzing effect. She became frozen within the veil of mockery that shrouded her every moment. There was no way in which she could begin to turn around the unyielding conditions and hope for a better tomorrow.

Her mind was straight, or so she thought. She felt she knew what was wrong – to the extent that she considered such irrelevancies. She knew what she wanted and she thought she had found a vehicle by which to right her ship, so to speak. *I just need to get these big, beautiful things out in public. The others will stop making jokes then. These babies will win over even Vice Principal Montgomery, that self-righteous bastard.* It took a week for her to scheme a scenario by which to lure the vice principal into her web, or more specifically into the down draft that flowed through her cavernous cleavage.

33

When one of the students smacked Ruthie's hand with a ruler while she slept through study hall, sleep that sounded by a lumber mill, Ruthie shot forth with a disconnected string of expletives as the red, stinging sensation crept up her hand and wrist. A cacophony of laughter erupted sending the quietude of the study hall into absolute bedlam.

Ruthie's abrupt response upon being pulled from the one place on earth where she was queen, curvaceous, lovable and highly desirable was an emotional eruption. The pasty-looking study hall proctor clutched at his chest, his mouth agape, eyes bulging and temporal veins swelling. The son of a preacher of some ill-defined denomination, the proctor gasped at the sound of the monosyllabic words Ruthie had spit out like castor oil. He bolted from his chair, his three-piece suit popping buttons as he rose. The man, who was a classic example of social maladjustment, struggled through the narrow aisle, his wire-rimmed glasses teetering across the bridge of his nose, his eyebrows arched toward his receding hairline and his mouth pitched in an exaggerated expression as if he had just extracted a gigantic popsicle.

"Shit, piss, fuck, bitch, hate, shit, and fuck you." Ruthie's proclamation, an unwitting gesture, and her only rebuttal to the whack on the hands hit the scrawny, uptight bible-thumper like a kick boxer's shot to the groin. He stood over Ruthie ponderously electing an appropriate response before clasping her ear lobe and literally dragging her bulbous form down the aisle of desks, out the door and into the small office occupied by the reigning head of the CJHS *Head of the Gestapo*, Vice Principal Montgomery.

"Thought I might see you again Miss Ross. But sooner than I expected, I must admit. Now what have you done this time you fat little bitch." Vice Principal Montgomery was not known for his tact or aplomb but rarely had any complaints from the parents – he got results and banged many a student into shape without them having to be sent to juvenile hall for incarceration.

"Shit, piss, fuck, bitch, hate, shit, fuck you."

"Well thank you. That clarifies everything. . . and shit, piss, fuck, bastard, hate, shit and fuck to you too young woman." After looking over something on his desk, extracting the glasses from his tarnished face and shoving a well-worn, saliva-soaked stump of a cigar into his teeth, he began a litany of possible outcomes for her behavior. "I think we can find a remedy for that cesspool of a mouth of yours." The Vice Principal gave Ruthie a shove down onto an unforgiving wooden chair across from his desk. As he continued his prolonged dissertation about civil society, its rights and wrongs, and his personal value system, Ruthie quietly undid the top two buttons to the bodice of her ill-fitting dress. The *twins* hiding underneath finally had an opportunity to creep out for a breath of fresh air, and be seen – their favorite pastime.

The cigar stump started to sag over Montgomery's lower lip; its last indication of smoke rising into his eyes and finally it dropped altogether onto a file atop his desk. His mouth dropped at about the same rate and nearly as far. For her part, Ruthie sucked in a little more air and pushed forward in recognition of the knowledge that the dropped cigar was the signal that the vice principal couldn't believe his eyes he was so enamored with the youthful protrusion of female flesh in so provocative a way. Ruthie was never prouder of herself than at this moment. She had overcome the onerous, villainous Mr. Montgomery and won his eyes and hopefully his hands and more. She'd heard the stories about where this could lead and this paramount symbol of authority was where she wanted to start. The bragging rights would be insurmountable.

For his part, dropping his cigar was a sign of disbelief all right – not so much at the size of Ruthie's chest but at the fact that she had seen fit to do this to him and here at the school where, if misinterpreted, could be the end of his long (and dubious) career. Ruthie represented a personal and institutional threat. She had to be removed. Now.

The minor commotion that had erupted in the small office sent Mrs. Dingle skating across the room as if there were wheels beneath her boxy orthopedic shoes. Without so much as a peck on the door to garner entry, Mrs. Dingle burst into the room, her eyes filled with horror and lack of understanding as to what was transpiring here in the hallowed offices of CJHS, hallowed to Mrs. Dingle at least. Upon her entry, Ruthie jumped to her feet and began to fumble with the buttons immediately as if she had been violated. "I hope you've seen enough, you. . . you dirty old man. Threatening me with expulsion if I didn't show you these, my precious and private femininity, that was uncalled for but you scared me." Ruthie feigned some tears and turned to snuggle her face into the bosom of the perplexed Mrs. Dingle, the school's administrative secretary and Mennonite spinster.

"I. I. I didn't do anything! I didn't tell her to do that! You nasty little bitch. I'll . . . ."

"You'll do no such thing Mr. Montgomery." Enveloping Ruthie with an arm around her shoulders, Mrs. Dingle had made a choice based on a long-standing belief that in her mind had just been corroborated.

The disbelieving vice principal stood there behind his desk astonished at what had just happened to him. Here, the bulwark of masculinity, the authority symbol of CJHS, and former football standout tackle, Class of '18 had just been emasculated by a dumpy-looking, brainless twit who happened to know how to play the game better than he did – age and apparent intelligence notwithstanding.

In the anteroom, Mrs. Dingle hastily took charge of the situation and explained to Ruthie that with Mr. Montgomery's temper running so hot it was most likely not very safe for Ruthie to remain – not just for the balance of the day but for the balance of the year.

"But Mrs. Dingle. My parents," stuttering she continued, "I mean my foster parents or guardians whatever they are will not understand. I can't go home. I can't tell them I was thrown out of school. It is so important to Mr. Radcliff, my foster father, that I get an education. I just can't end up nowhere."

37

"Sweetie, as I said, you really can't stay here. You walk across the street to Vellinger's Drug Store while I make a call or two and I will come join you and explain how we will work things out."

While Ruthie wiled away a half hour mindlessly thinking about Bob, thinking about being a princess, thinking about the natural allure that her body held for men, Mrs. Dingle called a close friend at the high school. Obviously, Ruthie was ill-prepared for high school, she realized, but she simply couldn't stay here. Her physical development would allow her to pass for an older person than she actually was – that could help.

About the time that Ruthie was sucking down a Coke and a third package of Hostess Twinkies and replaying the scene in Mr. Montgomery's office in her mind, relishing how excited she recognized him to be, Mrs. Dingle came charging through the drug store doorway with a big smile on her face.

"Ruthie. I have it all worked out. You're going to enter high school starting today. It won't be especially easy but I know the Radcliffe's would want the best for you and I am certain your heart is in the right place so a friend has agreed to bypass a whole list of rules and get you in."

"But Mrs. Dingle. . . I'm not ready. . . I. . . ."

"Don't you worry child. My friend explained that they have a whole shopping list of remedial classes and some special education people who can, and will, work with you to see to it that you understand what is going on. You'll do much better there than here. I promise you." She leaned down and gave

Ruthie a polite kiss on the forehead as she took the girl's hand and said, "come on. I'll drive you over to the school and get you introduced. Then I have to deal with Mr. Montgomery, that. . . that . . . ."

"Mrs. Dingle! . . such language. . . . "

Chapter 5
Frying Pan Into the Fire

Transitioning from junior high school to high school is like moving from Timex to Rolex. It is the difference between the prelude and the main event. Acculturation takes place in high school. Junior high had been for recognizing the imperfections of self and the nature of physical and emotional change as a result of puberty. High school was taking these realizations and casting them into the caldron of teenage society, stirring them around and finding out if you're the cook or the dinner. That's a tough pill for any kid to swallow but for many of the people who would comprise Ruthie's class, they had been together through grammar school and junior high school. For them, the next step was incremental. For Ruthie, however, it was an immediate slam dunk . . . that missed.

As with any class of students, there are smart one, dumb ones, those who push and those who drag. There are those who seek to challenge authority and those who are examples of future model citizens. Virtually all, however, had the intellectual capacity to be where they were – whether they applied it or not was always the key between success and failure. At least, though, they did have the fundamental tools and an academic history that got them to this place and time.

None of this, however, described Ruthie. She was thrown into the middle of the academic and emotional turbulence, without so much as an overnight's preparation psychologically. While her fellow students had the summer over which to prepare themselves, Ruthie had the amount of time that it took Mrs. Dingle to make the drive to the ivy-covered institution along the White River north of downtown.

While Ruthie sat on a hard wooden bench in the annex to the administrative offices, Mrs. Dingle did her best to explain the circumstances under which Ruthie was being *delivered*. For her part, Sharon Ozburne could only stare and grunt an occasional uh huh, uh huh. This was simply a case of providing a roof and four walls to retain the child until she was sixteen and could *walk* – glorified babysitting at best. The challenge for the school would be to keep Ruthie from doing any damage or having damage done to her. She was sounding increasingly like a nightmare in a two hundred pound package of unkempt clothes, unruly hair, misapplied makeup, and an attitude that could swing from one extreme to the other at the proverbial drop of the hat.

The meeting wrapped up with a professional friendship of twelve years starting to pull at the edges of the comfort zone. Sharon Ozburne was starting to feel that the friendship had been used to solve someone else's problem and she was now going to have to be stuck with it – come what may. The two parted company with the slightest of smiles being exchanged and Mrs. Dingle strode happily down the hallway toward the exit and her own emotional freedom. *She's now someone else's problem,* she thought, and the smile extended broadly across her face as she pushed open the door and walked into the sunlight. *It is a nice day after all.* The thought danced about in her head as a load had just been lifted from her shoulders. The conflict with Mr. Montgomery had been averted, no legal issues would drop from the sky, and sooner or later Ruthie was going to end up at MCHS. . . or juvenile hall. This was clearly a better course of action. *Gee, what a nice day it has turned into.* Mrs. Dingle, very pleased with herself, virtually danced her way to her Ford Falcon. As she turned the key, the decorous smile turned to a mild shade of grimace, the old Falcon was still a Falcon and it was not having a nice day.

Ms. Ozburne turned to Ruthie in the anteroom, a look of discomfort ensconced on her face. "Well, Miss Ross, it sounds like you're going to be an interesting addition to MCHS. You please sit there a while longer while I try to sort out how we're going to deal with you." Ms. Ozburne wheeled before a perplexed Ruthie could muster a response and dropped at her desk one hand curled around a pencil and the other propping up a head that had just begun to throb, mercilessly.

Ruthie tried to sit attentively on the hard, wooden straight back chair and remain as courteous as the circumstances would permit. However, even with the added cushion she had developed over the past two years the chair became increasingly uncomfortable and she began to fidget and squirm wanting desperately to go to the bathroom but Ms. Ozburne had been quite insistent in her direction to remain in place.

Ms. Ozburne was struggling with how to fit a new student into a class schedule that was already at midterm; she also looked for a person whom she could identify as an advisor, someone to provide a meaningful direction to the troubled young woman, and a list of subjects that would provide adequate stimulation but not be stifling. No answers were falling onto the blank sheet of paper as Ms. Ozburne had hoped. At the height of her frustration, the windowed-door to her small, utilitarian office burst open rattling the panes as it did so. "I have to pee!" shouted Ruthie who had begun to hold herself in an attempt to stem the obvious.

"Down the hall to the right, three doors. Then come right on back, I'll need to talk to you about your class schedule and what you're going to have to do." Ms. Ozburne's tone had been less than cordial but without intent. She had thought she had provided a succinct direction to an individual with a history of not taking directions with any degree of obvious comprehension. For her part, Ruthie didn't hear an informative direction; she heard a snapping verbal tone that sounded intimidating and resembling her father's direction to do this, do that.

"If this is what high school is like. . . it sucks." Ruthie had begun a dialogue with herself sitting in one of the enclosures in the girl's restroom. The assessment of the institution was punctuated with expletives, not always fitting into a logical discourse but they were powerful words. She knew. Salting them

43

into what one said when trying to make a point or get someone to pay attention was like slapping the person in the face and saying, hey pay attention! These attention-grabbers had been her father's contribution to her education and now because of his shortfall she was being cast into an abyss – she was afraid. . . terrified. She couldn't even pee despite the internal pressure until her mind lost its focus and she began to think about Bob. He always had a calming effect; she was so grateful for Bob and could not wait to get out of Ms. Ozburne's world and back to Bob.

Her business concluded and her discourse having run its course, Ruthie waddled back down the hallway to the straight back chair and continued her penance.

Ms. Ozburne finally concluded whatever she was doing and brought Ruthie in to explain how things would proceed including interviews with several teachers, an academic advisor, and one of the young girls from the office. As Ruthie rose from the crippling chair to follow a new set of order, a protracted and shrill sound deafened her. It seemed to drown all other sound and thought. It was the starting gun for the instantaneous thunder of nearly two thousand screaming, laughing, shouting kids who had just been set free – it was three o'clock and a veritable pardon from the warden.

At this point Ruthie was dismissed. . . as if that had specific meaning to the young girl who might have been considered an alien from another country or another world. She was clear across town from the orphanage and the Radcliff's house. No part of the MCHS neighborhood bore any resemblance to the young girl's mind – she had been transplanted by someone who had not thought through the conclusion of her actions. Mrs. Dingle had put Ruthie in an alien environment without a thought about getting her back to the part of town from which she had been taken. Ruthie began walking. There was worry in her mind but it was not oppressive – it slid in and out of focus. Intermittently, she entertained visions of how young boys at the high school would be wowed by her massive boobs and how she would use this power to improve her life. She kept walking.

At nine that evening she was still walking and quickly becoming overcome by the chill in the air. Finally, a passing police cruiser stopped and questioned her motives for wandering about in a strange neighborhood, underdressed for the time of evening and for the cool night air. The inadequacies of her responses got her a ride downtown to the station where she was asked why she hadn't called her parents for a ride home if she were in fact lost. "I have no money for a phone call," was her simple response. Furthermore, she had never committed the Radcliff's phone number to memory.

Mr. Radcliff upon arriving at the police station had permitted his fear and concern to channel into a mild rage. He couldn't find a solution to the questions as to where Ruthie was and why she hadn't come home from junior high and the more he stewed the madder he got. By the time he was face-to-face with Ruthie he resembled her father – the rage spilling over into a flamboyant verbal tirade about it being her fault that Ruthie had put Mrs. Radcliff into a case of apoplexy from worry.

Ruthie was less than forthcoming with responses adequate to the charges by the angry Mr. Radcliff and the more he raged on, the tighter she withdrew into her shell – the same shell she had used so frequently with her father and had set aside but had not discarded.

The rage had a cork put in it during the drive home. Mrs. Radcliff waxed between overpowering concern for what had happened to Ruthie, whatever it might have been, and her greater concern for her own peace of mind. She had been the victim of this day's misadventure. She had been the one most put out by whatever had caused Ruthie to wander the streets. The attempts to draw a distinguishable truth from Ruthie were so deeply hidden in the self-absorbed statements of anguish by Mrs. Radcliff that reality was not found that night. A severe rebuke admonished Ruthie for her lack of concern for the worries she had caused and then a punishment meted out that she would be restricted to her room for three days.

Four walls. No people. No Bob. This seemed all too familiar. It was the imprisonment her father had used to control his daughter. Here it was again.

Without explaining that she was now a high school student, overnight as it were, Ruthie simply asked, "what about school?"

"No school!" was the response by the still angered Mr. Radcliff. He saw attendance at school as a privilege, a plus, and fun, therefore, he was taking that away from her.

"But. . . ."

"No buts. You caused this and now you have to deal with it. You sit there for three days and think about the living hell you have put us through and then we will see what privileges you may or may not be entitled to." The door shut. A secondary sound made it sound as if it had been locked from the other side. She hadn't known there to be a lock on the door but maybe the sound was simply a fixation that added an exclamation point after being enclosed with the four walls as her only friends, once again.

"Oh I wish Bob were here. Bob. I need you Bob. Where are you Bob." The halting sound of her voice conceded to a choked, tearful refrain in which she pleaded with no one for the one thing that could make her time in the room bearable. She needed a friend. . . her friend. She needed Bob, but there was no Bob.

Chapter 6
Haunting and Taunting

Ruthie was essentially paroled on the third day following a stay in her minimum security incarceration with limited visitor privileges. Bob, wagging his tail furiously and looking markedly like he hadn't eaten for several days represented the only salutary embrace. He began licking Ruthie's feet as soon as he was able to dart into the room, his uncut claws scraping over the hardwood floors and skidding without traction as he banged into his true-blue friend. Next it was ankles, shins, hands, arms and finally "Mecca," he was licking Ruthie's chins, cheeks and nose.

Ruthie dragged her mixed-blood friend up to her chest and they embraced like friends who hadn't seen each other for years or possibly a relative who just realized he or she was going to be prominent in the will. Ruthie was now all smiles as she scratched her nails through the dog's flanks to send a signal of happiness. As she did, she could hear a distant call to arms, "you need to quit playing with that damned dog and get to school – junior high school requires your attendance and some effort, remember?"

With great trepidation, Ruthie slinked from her *jail cell* down the hallway to confront her foster mother and explain that she had graduated, more or less, and had moved up to high school – all fanfare withheld. She would also try to tie this event to the street wandering if it looked like Mrs. Radcliff had calmed down and could deal with it.

Just as there are many galaxies within the universe and they are millions and billions of light years apart from one another, so too is the difference between a teenage girl and her parents, in this case, foster parents. Ruthie's lack of articulation and communicative skills impaired by her brain trauma made the going that much tougher. She was lost for the best words to convey her message; she lacked the associative skills of analyzing and explaining events and consequences.

Somehow, she got through the foster parent crisis but realized that once she got to school she'd be expected, under duress, to explain herself all over again. Inevitability is, however, what it is.

That first day of high school, the following weeks and the next couple of years all blurred into a mental haze that rolled along over Ruthie, through Ruthie, and in spite of Ruthie. She had become a slow-moving target for marksmen of extraordinary skills. The girls made fun of her dresses, hairstyle, makeup, and awkward behavior and movements. The boys made their sordid little comments about her bulbous chest and salivated at the thought of globbing onto one for a Friday night's entertainment. The pack of jackals would tear into her virtue with fangs whetted with the taste of the kill. Mostly virgins themselves, they had the luxury of talking the game without ever having played the sport. . . or knowing the rules. This was perpetuated every day; it was every class break and before and after school – it was unrelenting. Ruthie could only close down as best she could and think of how one day she would make them pay for seeing and touching the twin orbs and, oh yeah, she also thought of Bob – her friend.

The most tedious time of all, however, was PE class, the compulsory gym class that obligated one to strip down in the locker room and don a pair of skimpy shorts and T-shirt. And while the shorts and T-shirt were quite snug, considering that her size, the real issue was getting out of her clothes and into the gym outfit, and later out of those clothes, into and through the showering routine, and back into her frumpy dress, rolled-up white socks and saddle shoes. Ruthie had body parts that she didn't recall ever seeing . . . even on the front of her body. She'd just reach as best she could, lather up and then let the warm water hiss and spray to remove the uncommon levels of perspiration. She quietly prayed, as the nuns had taught her, that one day the shower could rinse away the feelings of inadequacy that were implanted into her by the barbed-tongue girls who could find no shortage of distasteful comments to make about her weight. After her third or fourth towel, as required for her size, she realized that the girls were still lingering just out of sight jabbering about something and it could only be her. No one girl ever had the nerve to confront her directly. It took a small group to demonstrate enough gumption to hurl the barbs, point the fingers, and laugh a hideous laugh – such individuals only find strength in a group dynamic – they lacked personal courage within themselves. Therefore, it was always the pack mentality that attacked Ruthie as if she were a small lamb cut from the flock and ignored by the other sheep so as to be sacrificed and permit the others to live. . . and the wolf was always hungry.

High school presented an array of tortures for Ruthie. There were good days and there were bad days. On a good day, Ruthie simply went home on the bus in tears. A bad day was usually represented by a call to the police to take charge of the hysterically-charged screaming banshee and get her home. Even the cops left finger prints behind with their eyes – she could feel them right through her frumpy clothing.

Chapter 7

Ruthie-1 : Bobble Jo-Zip

T he mob mentality at MCHS held that Ruthie was two heart beats this side of being brain dead. Reality was somewhat different, of course. Ruthie was slow. Ruthie was socially inept, but Ruthie was a human being – one with a problem not of her making. Her ineptitude caused her to standout – she would have been the person dressed to the teeth in woolens at a nude beach. Complex issues were beyond her and the simpler things did take a little longer than for the hyenas who continued to snap their jaws at her hind quarters at every opportunity.

Ruthie was an easy target and what more could an insecure person look for in life that someone even more vulnerable than himself or herself. It was if Ruthie walked about the halls of MCHS with a large bulls eye target painted in red circles on both her front and back, particularly her back where most detractors found the prey the easiest to attack.

Jeremy Hammond seemed a little different than the vast bulk of the four hundred or so who comprised Ruthie's class at the high school. Rumor held that Jeremy came from a household of Christian Scientists. Because that didn't ring in as conventional Protestant, Catholic, or even atheist, it was held as *different* by most in the class. Being different was tantamount to becoming one of two things within the social construct of high school: a genius to whom no one could relate, or a social pariah. Different translated to being as important as another glob of dried-out chewing gum stuck to the underside of the desktop. Ruthie had become the center of attention at MCHS but Jeremy held the title of being last month's Double Bubble stuck to the bottom of a study hall desk – unnoticed.

Jeremy was content with the underside of the social circle; he could see in Ruthie the possible reversal of fortunes for notice by the in-crowd. Jeremy had the talent of being able to slink through the hallways at class-change time without ever being noticed. Sliding from one open locker door to another as if a purposeful exercise, his presence was equated with the open locker doors, not with those standing about talking as he quietly glided his way to the next class. His greatest achievements lay in his ability to arrive at class without having to confront anyone who could ask him if Albert Einstein was the pope in his church or if he wanted to be a camouflaged commando when he got out of school. He lived in the shadows but he could see into the light and the unenviable plight of Ruthie. He emphasized with her situation but in no way wanted to change rolls with her. He knew he was last month's chewing gum - that worked for him. Jeremy just kept his eyes open and his mouth shut. He empathized with Ruthie but could not quite see throwing himself under the bus that had targeted Ruthie. That wouldn't help Ruthie and sacrificing himself. . . well, what would that gain?

On the other hand, there was Bobbie Jo. Bobbie Jo Fundren was not like Jeremy in terms of maintaining an invisible profile. Bobbie Jo was not like Ruthie either. Bobbie Jo was out front – she was an absolute stunner, a "10" even for those who used an Abacus. She was the captain of the cheerleading squad and one of the principal *head-turners* in Muncie. While her test scores provided a complacent "C" average, she managed to parlay her smile and a few visual teases into a solid "B" average. No male student could seem to resist the opportunity to do her bidding, to be her counterpart in conversation or to be seated properly for her famous high kick during her cheerleader performance. "Oh, my heavens, when changing into my cheerleader outfit, I must have forgotten to put my panties back on." That was Bobbie Jo's defense when confronted by the Vice Principal who inadvertently caught her act during a particularly vigorous set of stunts to cheer up the boy's section during a basketball game. By the time Bobbie Jo had finished her charm routine on the Vice Principal he was practically begging for forgiveness for having had to talk with her. She was, after all, Bobbie Jo – the most loved student at the school. She had any and every boy she wanted, she manipulated the male teachers and she even had all the competition under control. While the other girls saw Bobbie Jo with eyes so envious they could conceivably throttle the little princess, they had elected as one to fall in behind her and take the overflow from her cup rather than fight against her.

Bobbie Jo handled her celebrity predictably. She could have quoted Muhammad Ali's line, "I am the greatest," but there was no need for her to vocalize the obvious in such a crass manner. It was there for all to see as if imprinted across her forehead in bold lettering. Instead, of self-aggrandizement, she simply strutted down the hallways in such a way that her tight little ass looked like a highly-polished diamond. Her shapely, tanned legs held the promise of wonderment. Her face seemed as if it had been brought to life by Michelangelo himself - it was framed by a flowing mane of blonde hair that hung to well below her shoulders and was blonde to the roots. Her choices of outfits and accessories were like exclamation point following bold statements from a dictator – they had their impact.

Bobbie Jo had it all and the promise of perpetuating her lifestyle right into and through college to to land the man with the greatest promise of providing for her. Bobbie Jo had a career path, of sorts, and no one stood in her way. She had only to think of what she wanted; and her will be done. Others anticipated her every need and so provided.

Ruthie, like everyone else, could see the star quality, the aura, that seemed to surround the presence of Bobbie Jo. Some adulated her very existence, some envied her success. Ruthie could have cared less. Ruthie had come to terms with the distinctions in their relative worlds to realize that there *was* Bobbie Jo and then there *was* Ruthie – opposite ends of a continuum. A friend, however, would have been nice. Someone to talk to, to share with, just to help make time less a millstone around her thick neck – that would have been a godsend. Bobbie Jo would never be that friend.

Tuesday had been a particularly painful day. The expectations in class had been onerous and taxing and that was followed by the obligatory laughing and pointing, teasing and harassing. Ruthie left the class, as was not uncommon, on the verge of tears that she fought back. On Wednesday, keeping in mind the debacle following English class the preceding day, Jeremy came up alongside Ruthie as she was moving from one class to another. "I'm terribly sorry that the others made fun of you in class yesterday. I felt awful about that." Jeremy was caught by a twinge of bashfulness at having had the courage to make the remark to someone he didn't actually know and to whom he had never previously spoken. Ruthie was dumbstruck. No one ever spoke to her. . . about her, all the time, but never with her. Her head swiveled toward the Jack Sprat look alike so caught off guard that someone had actually spoken to her she could not respond. Her mouth simply slumped into an expression of disbelief. No words came forth, her mind simply didn't work that fast. She simply stopped as if skidding to a stop at a red light, her mouth drooping open, and her posture hung forward as her eyes followed Jeremy, now the god-of-all-mankind, Hammond. She could have been zapped with a Taser and felt no less sensation than that which enveloped her body and soul at this moment. *Someone spoke to me!*

Thursday, and every day that followed, Ruthie actually made every attempt to dress neatly, apply her makeup correctly and begin to act more attentively than simply passing through life like a fart in a hurricane. The storm had hit her and a lightning bolt had burned through to her very core. It had only taken a few kind words to make a difference in her self-perception and outlook.

The relationship that followed Ruthie's efforts took off much like the scene at the Calaveras County Frog Jumping contest – a leap here, a leap there, seldom in the same direction and completely without predictability. Eventually, they both seemed to jump to the same spot, so to speak, and began an interlude of *intercourse* – they actually spoke to each other, infrequently, then from time-to-time, and finally on a constant basis.

Jeremy was not a show-stopper. His boney structure held his clothes limply with no particular muscular structure to fill the sleeves or chest. His hair was neatly combed, almost to a point of fastidiousness but there was a clump of strands that stood erect toward the back of his head where the part ended. His skin was almost shiny but with no stubble to suggest the arrival of manhood. The other side of the coin held that he also did not have acne, the prevailing trauma to most teenagers. His clothes lacked the labels for which there were great followings; they also lacked a crease to signify a precision to his appearance. His was a middle class family with enough income to clothe Jeremy comfortably but this was overridden by a value system that dictated frugality and practicality. No one was turned on by the sight of Jeremy Hammond strolling down the MCHS hallway. . . nor were they repelled. He was simply there, unobtrusively, quietly, and without voice. There was no way that he'd ever magnetize the eyes of the would-be starlet, Bobbie Jo Fundren. She was in a class all her own and mere mortals like Jeremy couldn't even develop meaningful fantasies about a girl that far out of their league.

Bobbie Jo didn't know the name of the geek that seemed to slide through the shadows and through the class-break crowds without being particularly evident to anyone. There was a buzz, however, that filled the hallway's air. It seemed that that grotesque thing called Ruthie had attracted the invisible, no-name guy. *How is that possible*, Bobbie Jo wondered. *How could this guy be attracted to her? If he is attracted to her, he can't be attracted to me. That simply isn't possible. What the hell is going on?*

Bobbie Jo didn't want Jeremy. She wanted every guy. She wanted them hanging about the hallways salivating as she strutted past. She wanted them to think about her when they were fumbling about trying to unsnap the bra of their girlfriends in the backseat on lovers' lane. She wanted her face, her body to be ever-present in their psyche when they used the word girl or woman or certainly when they used adjective like desirable, beautiful, knock out bod and so on. It wasn't one or two or even the whole football team. She wanted them all. They were the matchsticks she used to count by. How dare one slip through the cracks? Was he blind not to see her and worse still what could he possibly see in that grotesque form known as *Ruthie*? This simply could not be; it had to be ended. She would see to it.

Over the next couple weeks Bobbie Jo manipulated her siren qualities to try to bewitch the soul that had strayed from the flock. The harder she seemed to try, the more obvious it became and the less he seemed to be willing to respond. *What in the hell is wrong? I haven't lost it,* she told herself. *I've still got it, look at me. Who else in this town looks this good and the crowning achievement. . . I haven't had to give anything away to get what I want. These poor stupid bastards would never be able to get my legs open, not here, not now, not any time. It's that damn girl. . .* that's the problem. *What could she possibly be doing for this fool that he can't see what I've got is world's better?*

Jealousy had gotten so deeply under the thin skin of Bobbie Jo that it had become a serious distraction. She looked at the fool and shook her head. She looked at what the fool was looking at and shook her head. "It's time to teach that bitch a lesson," she ranted to herself while walking through the school's parking lot. "It ends now!"

Ruthie was ahead of her; she had just waved as Jeremy had gotten in his Nash Rambler and driven off. A smile danced about Ruthie's face like happy children playing at Christmas. It was a rather warm late-Spring afternoon, the sky held not a single cloud, not a wisp of a breeze. Beads of perspiration had popped out on Ruthie's forehead, her blouse had become damp and sticky but these minor discomforts held no meaning. Ruthie was in love with Jeremy and he had just told her how attracted he was to her. The world was finally taking shape, the planets were aligning and everyone seemed to speak the same language, war and disease no longer existed – only happiness prevailed.

"Hey! Hey, you," came the barking sound of a she-devil behind her, venom dripping from the fiend's tongue with each new biting sound. "I want to talk to you!" came the call to arms.

"Me? What could you possibly want to talk to me about?" replied a bewildered Ruthie sheepishly. The smile drained from her face and was replaced with a look of utter confusion.

"I want that guy." Bobbie Jo planted her feet apart, one slightly ahead of the other establishing a point of balance as if to embark on an athletic event or a fight. Her hands snapped down onto her hips and grasped the cloth of her skirt so tightly that her fingers rose to a bright red. "You have no right to him, no lock on him. I want him and I mean to have him." She began to move in a circle around Ruthie eyeing her from top to bottom, her salacious barbs dripping in a hateful harangue. When she was once again back in front of Ruthie she unleashed her final vindictive. "I've got everything any guy would want. This guy. . . this fool just hasn't had a chance to see for himself. When he does, he's mine."

It wasn't enough to degrade and taunt Ruthie and turn her one good day into another nightmare. Bobbie Jo had to go the extra mile to drive the stake through the heart of the person who was keeping her from having a perfect record: Bobbie Jo-everything : Everyone else-zero. She wanted to hear from the lips of this corpulent enigma. She wanted to hear precisely what

60

this girl thought she had that Bobbie Jo didn't. "Tell me. . . show me, what do you think you have that I don't?" she paused knowing full well that the challenge was hollow and would doubtless send this strange form of competition hurdling through the streets in tearful agony.

Defiantly Ruthie stepped forward. They were eye-to-eye and were almost in actual physical contact when Ruthie broke her silence. She began with a determined look on her face and then lifting her hands to the upper part of her dress she ripped downward quickly as her jaw set firmly at the same time. She spilled forth from the dress, her oversized breasts flopping out in plain sight. "He likes my tits, stupid. They're the greatest tits he's ever seen and look at you – you don't have any. You've got nothin' and I have these big beautiful things. He loves them and he loves me."

Bobbie Jo stood with her mouth hanging wide open, her eyes fixed on some blank point in space, not moving, not speaking for at least ten minutes after Ruthie strode toward her bus.

Chapter 8
Muncie is Middletown

To understand Ruthie it is necessary to put her into a proper frame of reference. If she is beginning to sound like a complete enigma, it is time to back up and look at the world around her. If we fail to do so, it would be akin to "ETs" trying to make sense about the human race by scanning the clouds of television signals we emit. Or perhaps, an alien might land in upper Manhattan and generalize about the human race by looking at life's conditions in Spanish Harlem. Maybe even closer to home in an interpretive sense, if the alien landed in Dingfud in eastern Kentucky and chose to interpret the intelligentsia of the human race as found at Dingfud, how would our species hold up to intellectual scrutiny?

Presumably, if the little "green men" that we fanaticize so much about are anything like the press they are given, they would have a common language or the capability to instantaneous interpretation of other communication beyond their own. Landing on earth would leave the hairless little buggers in a quandary with hundreds of languages spoken around the globe and the common lack of ability for one race or nation to understand the thoughts of the others. Landing in Los Angeles alone, would cause apoplexy for most of the bug-eyed greenies with some eighty-five languages spoken in the Hollywood district alone.

Enough for similes between Ruthie and the aliens that populate the heavens. Her world is divergent enough and she alien enough that it isn't necessary to paint her green and have her don two coal black eyes the size of dinner plates.

Ruthie, as has been said, was born and came to age in Muncie, Indiana. Nearly a hundred years ago, a team of researchers first stereotyped Muncie as the quintessential example of "middle America." Without belaboring the point, the researchers established measurable criteria to assess the social significance of lifestyles in Muncie to determine the extent to which it might reflect a common theme around the country. Muncie landed the title of "Middletown" as it was felt that it sat at the core of social, commercial, and industrial achievements of American culture. . . how we dealt with the social institutions that have been created to guide us as a society and how we interact with one another in the process. Someone involved in the continuing research efforts to view the social dynamic of the community would no doubt have a more finite and authoritarian interpretation of the results. We're going to say for the sake of argument that this loose interpretation is close enough.

Muncie, if you haven't as yet booked air fare to this seductive vacation destination is in east central Indiana. For those of you who tend to fly east to west or vice versa, Indiana is one of those states roughly in the middle of your flight. If you leave

San Francisco on a flight at one in the afternoon, look out the window at about four o'clock – it all looks pretty much the same so if you're seeing Illinois or Ohio it doesn't matter so much. Most likely you'll just see cloud cover but in the rare instance that Moses has parted the sea of clouds and you can see to the ground, Muncie will be a dark little patch among the sea of fields of corn, wheat and mostly soy beans.

If you have found Muncie by driving, chances are you're lost.

Muncie was an Indian, Chief Muncie to be more precise of the Delaware tribe. There's a tarnishing bronze statue to his memory standing somewhere north of the downtown area. The city fathers seem to hold the belief that the tarnished statue is a natural phenomenon of nature with the oxidizing of the metal and its resulting patina. There are others, however, who can rightly point to the number of drunken college students who have recycled their beer onto the accommodating war chief who is now completely incapable of fighting back. If there's the soul of the old chief residing within the edifice he must be as pissed off as he has been pissed on.

That brings us to the college students and the academic haunts known as Ball State University or within the drinking community as Fruit Jar U or Testicle Tech. Not a bad school as colleges go. . . but don't look for a student to walk about the campus trying to solve simultaneous equations on a slide rule as he hustles from one class to another. Better you sit back at the corner of Riverside and McKinley and count the number of students wearing sweatshirts that say Ball U. Much to the chagrin of the administration, some enterprising soul made the intellectual leap and has probably made a fortune out of humiliating the school. Ball?, you ask. . . . Well, the school was founded or funded or at the least financially floated by the Ball brothers – a family of five brothers who founded a company based on canning jars. Today their production focus is more along the lines of the aerospace industry than for the little farm wives who want to preserve pickled pig's feet, grape jam, or this year's crop of pigmy corn. But times change and finding a farm wife who still spends her days boiling down a batch of garden vegetables for preservation for future consumption is about as common as finding a millionaire in such a place. But wait! This is where David Letterman went to college and it is where Jim Davis went to college, the latter being the creator of Garfield the cat – both obviously with a stellar sense of humor but then what does it take to live in Middletown if not a sense of humor.

Actually talking about the students from good ole BSU is central to our discussion about Ruthie. Historically, and still to a very significant degree, Ball State has been and is a college for the training of teachers and holds a prestigious ranking among peer institutions in this domain. Far more women are teachers than men therefore by extension, far more of the students at a teachers' college are girls than guys. I think we've just defined one of the fundamental tenets of a party school – unlike cross state rival Purdue University that is predominantly male engineering students (who do, by the way, walk around the campus solving simultaneous equations on the slide rules hung from their belts and transcribe their findings with a pen found in their shirt pocket protector. . . lest we digress.)

Muncie is industrial – at least it was before the rust belt syndrome began to plague the Midwest like an infestation of locusts. With so many heavy industry jobs going off-shore, Muncie became one of those communities left in a technological backwater. Muncie had also been one of the way-stops for the migratory flock from the hills of Kentucky and Tennessee – a resulting culture clash was the net effect. It became an odd melting pot of sorts: home to those escaping farm life, those escaping the destitute poverty of Appalachia, and the traditional middle class, small town work-a-day types. Add to the mix the influx of roughly twenty thousand inbound college students from the rural areas and small towns of Indiana and you have Middletown.

This was Ruthie's Middletown. She had been the prodigy of a father who had been a Detroit-outlier and a mother who had come from the coal region of eastern Kentucky – neither had the word cosmopolitan associated with their legacy.

Had Ruthie been born in New York City, she would have fit in simply as a function of numbers. Had she been born in Cat Creek, Montana, she would have been nurtured by the whole community, all ten or so who call Cat Creek home. However, she was born in the middle of the country, in a middle-sized community, in a placed analyzed to be Middletown (America) and she had to find a way to come to terms with her identity and make a life for herself.

Chapter 9
Fruit Jar "U"

T he opposite side of Ruthie's "Middletown," the west side, held the largest institution in western Indiana – Ball State University. Fruit Jar U as it was affectionately called, or Testicle Tech by the more perverse, was not exactly an academic bastion, but one of the finest teachers' colleges to be found. Over time it continued to broaden its breadth and depth and achieve excellence. However, during Ruthie's day, BSU was more a fun place to go to school than one where an invitation to a Rhodes's Scholarship was a consequential outcome. During the sixties it remained a teacher's college which meant that it was populated to a large extent by young women which, in turn, meant that the guy's who matriculated at the university basically had a hunting license and could roam the campus like a one-eyed dog at a meat market.

Ruthie would see the coeds at the shopping mall, such as it was. Their tight young bodies pushing out through undersized sweaters became the quintessential targets for the male population of the campus. This was the first experience away from home for many. Given the campus location and its academic focus, a great many of the coeds came from small towns and farms. So not only were they effectively ripe for the picking they were also fruit wanting to be picked – many needed that "first time" experience. Ruthie looked these girls up and down. She was torn between a feeling of a wanton desire to be just like them and a seething loathing for what they had that she did not – nice clothes, provocative clothes and nubile, young bodies bursting at the seams to garner a public display.

Increasingly, the encounters with the BSU coeds led Ruthie to the practice of self-assessment in front of a mirror at her foster home. She was in her senior year of high school – not that she had logged four years of accomplished achievement, quite the contrary. She had filled space required by the State of Indiana and otherwise had no place else to go. Furthermore, no teacher seemed to want to hold her back so as to further assist with her education. Pass her along to the next poor slob seemed to be the modus operandi – someone else's problem.

If Ruthie left school, she would have had to work and there simply were no appealing jobs for a person of her unkempt appearance and excessive displacement. The longing looks into the mirror transfixed a mood and began to mold a pattern of belief in the woman-child.

Each prolonged encounter with the mirror seemed to produce the same result – a deepening pattern of depression. Unless Ruthie stood some distance away, the mirror was loathe to return her full image – she thought this not so bad. By lopping off both her left and right sides due to the all-too-narrow mirror, it was occasionally possible for Ruthie to see a transfigured image – one that was thin, lean, and appealing. However, the jowls became a give-away that the mirror could not eradicate. On the plus side, Ruthie's spirits were buoyed each time by the reflected beneficence that had been bestowed on her chest. The forty-four inch orbs that hung so pendulously blocking any sight of her feet and the intervening body parts became ever more the reason for self-aggrandizement. Much like the witch who uttered, *mirror, mirror on the wall, who's the fairest of them all?,* Ruthie, too, consulted the mirror for guidance as to how to put her best foot forward. . . actually, how to put her boobs forward to her benefit and sense of self-worth. They had served her well with Jeremy and managed to cause Bobbie Jo no end of consternation because her boobs had come between Bobbie Jo and her conquest for a 100% market share in the high school's male population. Bobbie Jo hadn't been happy with just the athletic heroes; her consort included the dweebs and dorks, the male teachers and even the school mascot. Only Jeremy had slipped through the net that Bobbie Jo had cast. Bobbie Jo considered Jeremy to be completely brain dead. The truth was that he had been a breast-fed baby and saw in Ruthie a veritable homecoming of sorts. They, her boobs, had functioned much like two gigantic magnets for the poor obsessed boy. That had passed, however, and like the other 99.9% of the male population he tripped over some sort of landmine that put him among the Bobbie Jo crowd. Ruthie was indeed alone now.

The loss of the one individual whom Ruthie could claim as a friend and, dare we say, admirer had pushed Ruthie over the edge during that senior year in school. Her truancy rate increased dramatically, her appearance saw an even further degradation but it was more an attitudinal issue than anything. She was lost. Not even Bob could now nuzzle up to her and turn her world around.

Days turned into nights; nights turned into days. She wandered, occasionally touching base for something to eat and a clothes change. There was the indifferent exchange with the foster parents, the ineffective stroke or two over the uncombed, dirty hair that framed Bob's face and then it was off again. Sitting along the embankment of the White River that bisected the city became a favorite warm-day activity. As an alternative there were the days that she'd push harder and walk across town to the edge of the college campus. It was much like a child pressing his or her nose against the window of a candy store. Like the child, Ruthie knew that the campus was not for her and she dared not enter. She'd surely be whacked across the wrists with the ruler as had been the favorite punishment of the Mother Superior at the orphanage. Still. . . it was somehow gratifying to peer into this other world, this domain of the "chosen ones." They seemed to have everything, clothes, good looks. . . each other. And Ruthie had nothing. The long walks proved to be exhausting but more to the point they were emotionally devastating. Yet she couldn't resist the temptation to look inside, as it were, to see what life could have been like. . . or might still be with a minor miracle or two.

Ruthie sat on the bus bench at the corner of McKinley and University, slouched into a frumpy, lazy posture, her eyes fixed on the entrance to the Talley, the on-campus hot spot where all the coeds and the coed-chasers collected in the afternoons. If her eyes could have been read like a message on a television screen, doubtless the message would have been one of envy and longing. But then out of the corner of her peripheral vision something caught her eye and broke the spell. A bright new yellow Cadillac pulled into the parking lot adjacent to the building in which the kids were all congregating. The car was very much out of keeping with the normal run-down, dilapidated hand-me-down cars driven my most on the campus and even the small over-aged sports cars driven by those with the highest sense of self-worth in the favorite fraternities.

Ruthie's focus changed to study the oddity that had invaded her highly successful attempt to conjure a psychological framework for self-pity and self-destruction.

Several of the male students, or they seemed to look like students she thought, approached the rolled-down window of the flashy car that was laden with chrome, broad white-wall tires and a hood ornament that appeared to be a buxom, naked woman leaning into the wind when the car moved.

One student after another seemed to come forward and then quickly disappear from the Cadillac as if it had a plague and a quick retreat would guarantee their quarantine from the contact. For the life of her, Ruthie could not establish a fix on what was going on at the big yellow boat that had floated into the lot

71

filled with Chevys, Fords, and derelict VW microbuses. It stood out like a cut and polished diamond mixed in with a handful of chunks of coal.

Curiosity being the keeper of Ruthie's keys, she shrugged once and then pushed herself off the bench, crossed the street and picked her way between the parked cars to see what lord it was who drove such a magnificent machine.

The necklace-laden dude behind the wheel appeared to not have a good sense of his national origin – he looked like a New York pimp bedecked in necklaces and rings seemingly of gold, a belt buckle the size a hubcap from a sports car and one gold tooth displayed prominently in the center of his tight-lipped mouth. He caught a glimpse of Ruthie approaching the car and hit a button; she stared in awe as the window seemed to magically disappear down into the door. She stood a foot or so back from the car, peering down at the dude. There were little packets of folded paper piled on the seat next to the dude's leg. He turned in Ruthie's direction, "Hey, baby. Suuup?" As he smiled, the gold tooth displayed an inset diamond gleaming beneath the pencil-thin excuse for a mustache.

Ruthie was certain she had now seen it all: a car of glorious proportions and appointments, more gold than could possibly be held in Fort Knox, and diamonds scattered about the devilishly-handsome stud behind the wheel. Instead of responding to the non-question, Ruthie inexplicably let a sigh slip between her lips, a long sound that seemed to be emitted not from her lips but from her soul.

Once she regained some level of her composure Ruthie leaned her two elbows across the window sill of the passenger door. Her shoulders sunk a little as she protruded her head inside to get a better look at the magnificent car with its white leather everywhere, the really cute fuzzy dice hanging from the mirror, the knob on the steering wheel with an inlaid picture of a naked woman and the most handsome man she had ever seen. As her eyes took in the sights, a little light went on in the dimly lit recesses of her mind. *Hey! Here's a catch! And what have I been telling myself about how to find a guy? What is it I have that any guy would kill to get to?*

Ruthie looked down quickly to see that her top had fallen away and the dude was getting the twenty-five cent tour of Ruthie's potential playground. She quickly decided that if the twenty-cent tour had so effectively captured his eyes, what would the fifty-cent tour produce? What about the dollar tour? Acting on impulse, she popped off the next button down on her top, staring as she did so at her own breathtaking display. Visions of what might be had already begun to dance through her head giving her a giddy feeling, a playful sense of an I-dare-you attitude. Now the dude's eyes were riveted and he had to make adjustments in the way he was sitting as the twin orbs were demonstrating their potential to their fullest.

A student seemed to pop up out of nowhere at the driver's window. "Hey, man, you got a dime bag there?"

The dude started to reach in next to his leg to accommodate the kid's purchase but his eyes strayed from the seat where the little bags of junk were piled and they affixed once again on the mammoth display of pulchritude that was now the new Ruthie – the self-assured Ruthie who had 'em and intended to use 'em. "No, man, just sold my last. Ain't got none left. Maybe next time, huh?" The dude smiled a tight-lipped grin at the boy. He didn't intend to waste the display of the diamond tooth on some college dweeb, he'd save that for Miss Big Tits on the other side of the car. The student began a tirade of four-letter words, spun on his penny loafers and marched off in his chinos and button-down collar shirt. The dude didn't even see him go, he was too focused on some serious love potential hanging through his window.

"Baby, why don't you just bring those big beautiful things with you, climb on in here and I'll show you what this sweet machine can do. I'll show you what the car can do also." That flew past Ruthie like ducks headed south for the winter but he belted out a continuing series of guffaws believing that his sense of humor was second only to his good looks and studly qualities.

When Ruthie had settled into the rolling palace, a pre-eminent symbol of waste and poor taste, the dude stomped on the gas pedal leaving a double patch of black rubber down the length of the parking lot aisle as he steered with his left hand and quickly thrust his right straight into Ruthie's top.

It was the first time that someone had actually touched her and it sent electric wave after wave of excitement pulsing through her chest, down to her pelvic region and to her mind as

well. She had effectively lit up like a Christmas tree and responded to his touch, to any bystander, as if she had actually had
an orgasm. She was alive. He was the consummate sex dog and
she wanted a lot more.

She would get it.

Chapter 10
Better Living Through Modern Chemistry[*1]

Betwen being strung out on his own product and the not-infrequent drunken stupor that possessed his soul, The Dude ravaged Ruthie's body in true Bacchanalian fashion. He was all over her like the fur on a muskrat, beginning at his two favorite zip codes and then proceeding south before returning to his the two planets he loved to call home. There was nothing loving or lovable about The Dude. He had a thirst that had to be quenched and he drank freely and frequently, usually while roosting in the small trailer he called home on the southern outskirts of town. And while The Dude saw himself as the consummate ladies' man, a princely creation, the reality was that he couldn't pick up a good looking whore with a handful of fifties. Ruthie was a godsend for the spindly offspring of two cousins from eastern Tennessee.

The Dude hadn't quite finished school before he found his calling. The fourth grade had proved taxing enough and there was absolutely no incentive to go for five – so the fourth grade had been the bottom line on his resume. Now at twenty,

---

[*] Formerly Dupont's advertising slogan

the product of a limited gene pool was at the top of his game –
he had a flashy car, money in his pocket, and a pair of honkers
he could grab on to when the mood struck him. To ensure that
the honkers were his and his alone to game with and at any hour
of the day or night, after a minimal amount of coaxing The Dude
convinced Ruthie to move into his wheeled palace – a twenty-
foot Airstream. As homes go. . . a twenty-foot Airstream travel
trailer doesn't connote a strong sense of success, stability, or anything much beyond flightiness, insecurity, and poor white trash.
At a minimum, when two individuals crowd into the one hundred sixty or so square feet there wasn't much space to have personal differences. This was bad under the best of conditions, but
The Dude did not represent the best of conditions. He had
proved to be a problem in the womb and certainly ever since he
pried his way out prematurely from a mother who had left him in
an alley wrapped in a flannel shirt on a chilly November evening.

The Dude had a rather inauspicious beginning and never managed to rise above this unfortunate entry into a world that
didn't have any apparent use for him. It wasn't that The Dude
became a tough - his spindly arms, concave chest and flapping
ears earmarked him as a loser of grotesque proportions. Despite
his physical shortcomings, despite his lack of wherewithal financially and intellectually, The Dude managed to develop an attitude . . . from where, no one could quite comprehend, but an attitude nonetheless.

The Dude's strength socially came from his shortcomings. He had no regard for himself or for anyone else. He'd do what he had to to others to make his point or get his way. Fortunately, no one had ever (as yet) approached The Dude to undertake a hit – although it most likely would have fallen into his repertoire of job skills. It was no surprise when a carload of punks from Indianapolis had ventured into Muncie, some sixty miles northeast of "Indy," "Indian No Place," or "Nap Town," depending upon your jurisdictional prerogatives. They came to Muncie, rampaged through the local watering holes, hooted and hollered at every girl walking down the street and otherwise made complete fools of themselves from their '55 Chevy – all windows down despite the weather.

Considering what the carload of troublemakers had in their trunk, a low profile would have made good, common sense. However, as is the case with such people – it was sorely lacking. On pulling into the parking lot at Maxie's, a bar frequented largely by Ball State students, the first person they encountered was The Dude. While the witless quartet wanted to peddle some of their "smack" for a quick buck, then roost in Maxie's so as to act as a beacon to which all the dazzling coeds would flock, they also wanted to find a local distributor.

Enter The Dude.

The reason for The Dude to be at Maxie's, several years before his chance encounter with Ruthie, was quite similar to that of the witless quartet: he intended to give the coeds every opportunity to see what they hadn't as yet had a chance to enjoy and then he'd see to it that he delivered. Unfortunately, he didn't have two quarters to rub together with which to buy a beer and was wandering through the parking lot looking to hustle some naïve student into believing that he could get them in even if underage. . . but it would cost them.

Seller, meet buyer. Buyer, meet seller.

The four clueless individuals gathered around the rear bumper of the '55 Chevy had been cut out of the same cloth as The Dude. Somehow in this caliber of low-life there is still a unique quality of entrepreneurial spirit that transcends logic and the comfort zone of those who work hard for a living. The songless quartet didn't find their sale in The Dude but they did find a very willing participant in their business. There had been one caveat that dictated how the issue of trust would be accommodated in their business dealings: The Dude would get a .38 slug through the left eye if he ever screwed his partners and made off with any of their *bread* or product. The Dude assured him he was cool with that aspect of their arrangement as it simply didn't pertain to him – he was a stand-up kind of guy and could be trusted to take their product to market for them, return their *coin*, and never interfere by messing up the deal. Once all the handshakes had taken place and the .38 removed that had been held up to The Dude's left eye as a reminder of his contractual obligations, a large box from Kroger's grocery was shifted to the trunk of The Dude's rust-laden old car.

No one had ever seen so many yellowing teeth hung from the driver's window as The Dude buzzed down the street as happy as a clam.

The Dude lived up to the terms of the deal with the four morons from Indian No Place and made a bundle of money for himself. The .38 had been a thing of the past. They made money. He made money. In no time he had moved up to the shiny, bright new yellow Cadillac, a gold tooth with an inlaid diamond and an ever-present erection as he hunted the streets surrounding the campus looking for naïve strays to bag. That is what had led him to Ruthie.

Ruthie and The Dude came together through not dissimilar paths in life. In a way someone might say that they had been meant for each other. Ruthie certainly felt it so and for The Dude, it was all about Ruthie's rack – lookin', fiddlin', and taking a zillion Polaroids. Ruthie had been uptight about the Polaroid process, it was new to her. She didn't mind showing off the mams, they were her primary source of pride. . . hell, they were her only source of pride and then only if you valued quantity over quality. Eventually, however, the still teenage Ruthie was posing for The Dude's prurient interests indoors, outdoors, wherever the mood struck The Dude. The catch was, he had to pump Ruthie sufficiently full of his product that it knocked the edge off – that last remaining aspect of common sense, and morality as hammered into her by the Mother Superior. When Ruthie got high, she managed to undertake no limit of vulgar acts to please her beau, The Dude. He was happy. He must surely love

80

her, she reasoned. He was all over her all the time and he loved what she had. It had to be love – her first real love and it would last forever, she knew. Anything this good could have no end. Ruthie was now high so much of the time that any sense of reality had been lost. There was no longer a base, a ground zero. Everything floated in good times from one trip to another as she dropped acid, shot heroin, snorted cocaine and chased it with cheap liquor. The Dude had been very willing to please her; it was a balancing act. He gave what she needed and took what he needed. . . and still hadn't had to deal with the business end of the .38.

Early in 1967 a change came to the daily agenda of cruising the streets looking for the weak and defenseless with whom to make a drug sale. The Dude's trailer got a visit from the police, not with knowledge of his drug sales or the drugged-up whore just feet away splayed across their waterbed. The cop was there to notify The Dude that he had not responded to several notices and this was his last chance to do so before being arrested.

Without hesitation, The Dude acknowledged his agreement and took the summons and thanked the officer realizing that he had just managed to slip by a major arrest from the witless cop. As he sat on the edge of the waterbed, the naked Ruthie, in a haze, sloshed her way across the stained sheets and pressed the two mountainous orbs against the back of The Dude's neck as she enveloped him in her arms. Slobbering, her eyes half opened and completely out of focus, she managed a, "what is it hon?"

The Dude didn't read all that well but he did manage his way through the first part of the official-looking document that began, "Greetings." Two days later, The Dude had managed to make his way to the federal building in Nap Town to take a physical exam for entry into the Army. He had been drafted.

The Army had come to understand by 1967 that they needed some "cannon fodder" and guys like The Dude would fill the bill nicely.

The cold, gray room in the basement of the federal building held a series of compartmentalized functions that processed draft candidates through the various stages of the draft physical examination. All the young men in their chinos and button-down collar shirts stood in stark contrast to The Dude. They could read, think, and reason. The Dude could deal.

The first challenge to The Dude's ability to deal came during the first line-up. While the others were scrubbed and shiny for their appointment with "the man," The Dude stood out in line with his ill-fitting, stained-at-the-fly pants, rag-tag shoes, and disheveled shirt replete with smudges, beer stains and lipstick. What caught the eye of the examiner, however, was the messages The Dude had painted, not wrote or printed, but painted on his shirt. Around the collar he had painted the statement, "abolish the draft." On the breast pocket he had painted, "abolish the war." The messages seemed to be the catalyst to garner The Dude some private time with the hulking sergeant who lumbered through the room to personally escort The Dude to another location.

After some counseling, The Dude's next appearance was in another line-up. This time, like all the rest, he stood in a line in just his undershorts – heavily yellow-stained in the front and streaked in the back. This time the examiners found that The Dude had painted in red paint on his chest, "does this look like the body of a killer?" At this nexus, they just shook their heads and proceeded to the final phase. "Okay gentlemen, drop your shorts, spread your legs, and bend forward." The call from the doctor with the small flashlight had preceded his hurried pass down the back of the line. What he could expect to find at that speed and in such a location was anyone's guess, however, he did find one anatomical oddity that called for the hulking sergeant once again. The Dude had painted, actually he had Ruthie paint, "fuck – Army."[2] One word to each cheek – had been enough to gain the kind of attention his ego seemed to crave. He was singled out, dragged from the line with his shorts acting like loose-fitting ankle cuffs. The Dude wasn't seen again.

The Dude most likely became worm food in South Vietnam once Charlie had shot the slow-witted soldier countless times.

. . . and once again Ruthie was all alone. This time, however, she had been left with a major drug addiction and no way to tap a source. From what had become her twenty-foot

---

[2] *Exact, actual experience observed by the author during his own draft physical.*

trailer-home, she would have to find a way to use her one and only asset to make some money to buy a fix today. . . and tomorrow . . . and the day after . . . and so on.

Chapter 11

Life As a Parasite

The Dude hadn't been good to Ruthie, but sadly, she hadn't really noticed the difference. Despite the swearing, the backhands across the cheek, the drunken revelry and the delusional drug-induced interludes, Ruthie remained enraptured by the simple fact that there was someone on the face of the earth interested in her. . . for some reason. It didn't matter what the reason, it didn't matter that she'd had used her only ticket, the twin orbs, to land the attention. She had the attention, someone to whom to cling. It was a happy time for her. Gone were the days of having to listen to "life lessons" as preached by the over-lording, state-appointed guardians. No more angels and demons lectures by the towering Mother Superior. One regret: Bob had gotten left behind in the blur that had been the change in her life. The poor little dog probably had the same withdraw feelings that Ruthie had herself when Bob crept into her mind.

The Dude had replaced Bob. He had replaced the Mother Superior. He had replaced the Radcliffe's. He had even replaced the distasteful memory of that uppity bitch, Bobby Jo. But now The Dude was gone. After leaving for the physical exam in Indianapolis, he had not returned. After what seemed an eternity, a post card arrived with a terse message. It had to be terse as The Dude's ability to write hinged on his inability to spell but the message got across nonetheless: *Army life sucks. I'm at a place called Fort Polk. Luzyanna sucks, hot and stick-ee. Goin' to Vietnom I gess. The Dude.*

The news was bad, devastating in fact, but it was a post-card addressed to her – she cherished it and showed it around to other trailer park inhabitants. Bad news translated as good news can carry a conversation only so far and even the winos that populated the area began to steer clear of the big-chested chick that made no sense.

Even before the food ran out or the last of the Tequila sucked dry, the issue quickly became one of the need for a fix. With The Dude gone, the source was gone but her need was ev-er-present and demanding like a screaming bitch holding a skillet ready to crack your skull. Fortunately, the moronic quartet from Indy showed up after a week to download a shipment of their product onto The Dude for his street distribution. As per usual, they walked into the trailer without knocking and began pushing their way through the piled refuse that was home to Ruthie. Startled sufficiently to arise from the near delirium in which they found her, naked, splayed across the water bed as if in a dream, Ruthie jumped off the bed clutching at herself – first to cover her top, then her crotch, then her top again before a little light went on in her head.

"Hi, guys, The Dude's not here." Pausing and looking each of the disheveled truants over from top to bottom and wiping a smirk onto her face to stop a little drool from the corner of her lip, she continued. "I need some stuff. I need it now and to make it interesting for you, I'll do all four of you, at once if you like."

Malcolm, who liked to go by the name of Skid Marks due to the serious dislike for his name, said point blank to her face, "I don't do fat chicks."

Armando was apparently not as discriminating. "Go wait in the car Skid. We'll be out in a little while." Immediately they began stripping down and pawing Ruthie as they pushed her back on to the waterbed which sent a near-tidal wave from foot to head of the bed. In one of her more lucid moments, Ruthie had the presence of mind to clamp her legs tightly around the head of Buddy the apparent leader of the group and cut a deal for a continuing supply in exchange for whatever fun they wanted to have.

Buddy, who was most likely a clinical example of a sex addict agreed to the terms – they were terms that would be easy to fulfill. Ruthie would have her continuing supply of junk and the attention of three guys, not just the one. She was forced to do things and assume positions that she had never even thought of even with the strange perversions of The Dude. While such acts seemed strange at first, they became routine quickly enough and ultimately a source of overwhelming pleasure that was anticipated from one week to the next.

Other than letting Ruthie finish a half-eaten Big Mac and the dregs from a bag of fries, there was no food to be had and drugs and sex were not enough to sustain her. Even Ruthie with her diminished capacity had enough common sense to realize that she had to get out of the trailer and find some food, find some money, and perhaps even find a life.

Only so much life can transpire in a twenty foot trailer. The TV was on the fritz, the only music was that played overly loud by the Oakie in the next trailer down so there were countless hours of emotional agony, soul searching, thinking, longing, and crying.

Through the hours and days of self-pity a plan emerged from the limited options available to the societal anachronism. She had weighed the possibilities of getting a job, returning to live with the Radcliffe's, and begging at a major street intersection. Amazingly, Ruthie's self esteem while seemingly nonexistent excluded the begging option. Furthermore, she realized that a return to the Radcliffe's was out of the question. She had left without notice and had now been gone long enough that they had probably forgotten of her very existence. She had ignored attempts by interlopers to get her to return to the Radcliffe's and it was now a veritable impossibility. Sadly, the only other option on her plate was getting a job. While this wouldn't seem like a "deal-ender" for most people, Ruthie had never worked and had absolutely no marketable job skills. Even flipping burgers at McDonald's seemed like a high-end option.

Apparently, when all options are honestly exhausted, God is known to intervene in the lives of people without hope, particularly for those who had been touched by misfortune that rendered them beyond society's norms, as in brain damage. Sitting at the miniscule Formica-covered table Ruthie flicked a finger at an errant cockroach that had wandered onto the table for a smorgasbord of the leftover food bits. So startled was she from her concentration from playing "kick-ass" with the cockroach that she hadn't noticed a rap at the tin door. Startled, her finger flicked into the open air above the hard-charging beetle.

A lady introduced herself as Mrs. Przybylinski from the Department of Social Services. Ruthie stared open eyed at the middle age woman in the manly pants suit whose hair was pulled into a tight bun atop her head. Ruthie had never heard of the Department of Social Services and she was still focusing on the name the woman had given; it had sounded like so much gobblie gook, a mouthful of sound without meaning. "May I come in?" asked the woman in an accent that sounded American enough to Ruthie regardless of whatever the hell she had said her name was.

"Sure. Come on in. . . but what do you want?" Ruthie looked about her limited living space as the woman stepped up and entered the small trailer. "Pardon how things look. I haven't been myself lately, not since my boyfriend got drafted into the Army."

The woman looked about the premises as if a troop of lepers had just departed. Ruthie used her forearm in one long swipe to clear off the table top. "Sit down." She feigned a smile not knowing why the woman was there but certain nonetheless that the woman represented the authorities and would be taking her into custody because of her drug use.

"Ruthie. . . may I call you Ruthie?" asked the social worker.

"Sure. Everyone does." Ruthie smiled a tenuous smile in an attempt to soften what she was sure would follow. She shifted awkwardly in the chair, not so much because the plastic covering had been ripped from front to back and the batting protruded but because she was waiting for the shoe to drop – more bad news in a life that defined bad news.

"Ruthie, some of your neighbors have provided your name to. . . . " Mrs. Przybylinski was cut off immediately before she could go any further.

"Look, Mrs. Pruz, Priz, Pr, whatever, I'm not a bad girl. I've done nothing wrong. Those guys that come over are friends of my boyfriend and they just come to visit to console me."

"I'm not here about that Ruthie," the woman continued. "I'm from the welfare agency and after your neighbors had suggested that you might be someone who should be covered by our organization I got to checking into your background dating back to your infancy. You've been through a lot," she paused clearing her throat and peripherally catching sight of the returning cockroach, "yes, you've been through a lot and it would appear that you could use some help."

The executioner's axe had not fallen; Ruthie was relieved. Beads of perspiration had popped out across her forehead and her eyes bespoke a troubled, frightened soul. Immediately, she slumped from her uptight, rigid posture and her lower jaw dropped as she did. Her countenance in no way bespoke an image of comprehension of what the woman was talking about, but it did not connote a threat.

"I should tell you also that we are aware that you have a drug problem and we have no intention of providing state funds, regardless of how much your living conditions might require, for use for purchasing drugs for you to use. Therefore, to qualify for a monthly stipend you will have to submit yourself to a rehabilitation center to get cleaned up." The woman looked up from her notes only to see an impassive expression facing her. The message had been in two parts and it had been simple yet the young girl seemed confused. Mrs. Przybylinski realized that her presence had been appropriate. Here was a lost soul incapable of the most fundamental needs for her own survival.

"If you'll pull a few things together, someone will be here early this afternoon to take you to the Charles Street facility where you will live until you're through the program." Still, a blank stare was the only response. "Do you understand, Ruthie?

After a long pause and another flick at the cock roach Ruthie looked up and smiled. "Uh huh. But. . . " she staggered verbally to put her thoughts into words. "Is there someone at this facility who will play with these?" Ruthie pulled open the top of her blouse to display her only two remaining friends on the planet.

Dumfounded, Mrs. Przybylinski stood abruptly and took the two steps to the ill-fitting outer door. Over her shoulder she reiterated her directions. "Please be ready by two; someone will pick you up."

Ruthie stood and watched the befuddled woman stomp back to her green-over-white Studebaker shaking her head from side to side.

Ruthie looked down at her massive chest hanging from the front of her open shirt, "I don't think she liked us, what do you think?" Ruthie actually paused at the door before returning to the ever-present cockroach as if waiting for a response from the twins.

Chapter 12
The Pain of Sobriety

As anyone who has been through the process can tell you, cleaning up after succumbing to drugs for numerous months is anything but a slam dunk. Ruthie was by no means an exception. In point of fact, it was most likely more arduous for her than for the average drug abuser. She had no support system upon which she could fall back for encouragement and consoling words of advice. Even the most obvious down-and-outers had someone resembling a relative who would come in once a week, smile a lot, thank the abuser for making the effort and shower the individual with a deluge of platitudes about how this was critical and it would turn his or her life around.

The Radcliffe's were still so incensed that Ruthie had abandoned their home and their efforts that they chose to refuse the invitation by the center's director to periodically make an appearance so as to help their foster daughter. The Radcliffe's, on the other hand, were always very quick to point out that she was a "former" foster child; she had chosen to abandon them – not the reverse. So once again in her life, Ruthie had no one. . . not even Bob whom the Radcliffe's had confessed to the center's director they had had put to sleep. The dog had not been sick. They didn't want it or the reminder of Ruthie that it fostered.

Over several months Ruthie was in and out of the program, on drugs, off drugs, friendly, alienating. Her mood swings were radical from humble, quiet and sometimes simply non-responsive to boisterous and even threatening. This was not who she was; it was the devil that had taken up residence in the soul of a weak person, a really weak person. Her perception of reality did not extend to the nation or the American society, nor even the community of Muncie. . . not even to the microcosm of the trailer park. Her world was essentially within her reach. Doubt-less her vision had the capability to see beyond but her focus was within constantly lamenting the loss of The Dude. It was as if she were in a cocoon and had been placed there involuntarily. It was clear that she was overjoyed when someone was able to break that barrier such as had Bob or The Dude. . . even the four gang bangers from Naptown had awakened something in her but everyone else was held outside. To use a common expression, they were on the outside looking in would not be appropriate. They, the others beyond The Dude and the gang bangers, were on the outside not wanting to or bothering to try to look inside. Ruthie had problems; they had their own. Ruthie's problems would remain Ruthie's problems.

As with all the women in the program, they slept in a common dorm for females; there was a counterpart facility for men on the other side of the building. A military-type discipline was exacted to have the women maintain a small cupboard with their belongings and keep their bed made when not being used. Their lives were reasonably-well regimented in terms of the time to rise and the time to go to bed, time for counseling sessions, three meal times each day, several supervised outings, exercise and then filler which was used by most for chit-chatting among themselves.

Ruthie moved through the process like an automaton – without smiling, without conversation, without apparent understanding. She was simply there and going through the motions. It was a necessary evil if she was to get a check from the state so as to buy food. . . and possibly some vodka. . . and maybe a hit or two. She still hadn't differentiated the distinction between good and evil, cause and effect, or possibly even right from wrong. Generally speaking, however, she got through each day without incident, without offending others, without inciting riots with her temper, and without gaining anything positive to bolster her self-perception. She had no enemies, but she had no friends.

It was approaching midnight. The women's dorm sounded like a sawmill and ambient light almost non-existent. It was a late-Spring evening; the air was still and hung like a stagnant cloud throughout central Indiana. The only scent, a demonstrable suggestion that some of the clinic's sisterhood hadn't showered before collapsing into the let-me-forget-now world of sleep. No stirrings, only the ripping sound of the female nasal passage as the majority of the inhabitants tried to sleep through the ever-present pull back from the drugs.

Ruthie, like the rest, was tired and her body perplexed by what it needed and what it was being given. The push and pull that cried out from within her internal organs was heard clearly by a mind that had long since made a conscious decision to concede when such a challenge arose.

The concrete block walls of the forty by one hundred foot dorm room lined along each of two walls with metals cots were silent witnesses to the pungent odor that permeated the entire dorm room. The bouquet offered by women from the street, not accustomed to showering on a regular basis, had a distinct take-notice scent.

There was no moon at this time of the month and only a small amount of ambient light from some far away street light invaded the near total blackness of the dorm room. The only sounds were that of an errant dog yapping a couple blocks distant and the intermittent sound of what might have been a sawmill, the snoring of two dozen women who filled the dorm to capacity.

The lights had been extinguished at ten and the final chitter-chatter had finally culminated sometime before eleven.

Ruthie lay still, her mind racing among a dozen topics, some relevant to her recovery and some of absolutely no consequence – just vacant passages through the neural activity of her mind. Her eyes were open, then closed, then open again. She was tired but the remaining chemistry in the cells of her body kept sending confusing signals as to what she should be doing. She tried to sleep but she missed The Dude; she missed Bob.

As she thought about The Dude and what he did for her and to her a tingle deep within her groin sent a pleasant sensation, a warmth with vivid images of the fun they had had – *damn that Army anyway*, she thought. But rather than focus on the loss of The Dude, she let the tingle continue to pervade her system.

When that feeling seemed to cup one of her breasts as real as if The Dude were there, she let a smile envelop her face as her eyes tightened in anticipation of what The Dude would do next. The feeling turned her even warmer when it felt as if The Dude were there licking and sucking as he so commonly did, no matter where they might be. Instinctively she reached a hand out in her near-sleep state to pull The Dude's head tighter against her knowing that this was simply a prelude to what would evolve into a wonderful dream with which to fill her night.

Ruthie's hand slid through the hair of Deborah (pronounced D-bore-uh) who now had her lips affixed to Ruthie's bosom; Ruthie pulled her closer.

Slowly a light seemed to go on in Ruthie's less than nimble mind and she shot upright to see what had been happening. The light didn't permit a meaningful level of eye contact between the two girls. Deborah couldn't read a reaction from Ruthie's eyes but she continued to stroke and massage and tweak at the potential source of pleasure she had admired for the past two weeks but had been afraid to do anything about.

Without over analyzing the situation, Ruthie contented herself with the reality that her magnificent mams had done it again. She had been right when at the Radcliffe's she'd stare into the mirror and find her image so enticing. This situation was different than she had ever expected or certainly ever sought, but it felt good and it felt good to have someone no matter how or whom. She laid back, pulled the sheet aside, closed her eyes and pulled Deborah's head back to her chest. Had there been sufficient light Ruthie would have seen a smile on Deborah's face so profound that one would have thought she had just won the lottery.

The limited sexual performance followed each night during the remaining period of internment for each of the girls. They limited their public exposure to avoid official conflict with the program administrator and the jeers and taunts by their fellow dorm mates.

After a month or so both were out of the program and seemingly clean having been through the methadone withdrawal program and painfully lived to tell about it. During "recess" breaks they would chat in the courtyard and began to make plans for the life that would follow their release.

The trailer was still there. It appeared that either a derelict or a raccoon had taken up residence during Ruthie's absence. It was a wreck of monumental proportions but the presence of Deborah seemed to kindle a new spirit in Ruthie, one that had her taking greater responsibility for the appearance of the trailer and for her own appearance. Deborah never slapped Ruthie. She didn't spend the evenings gargling beer and farting and swearing like a sailor in the Philippines. There weren't even sessions with the Polaroid just quiet evenings spent in embrace and soft talk. They would walk and talk. They would shop at the market and talk. They lay together in bed free of any bond of clothing and they would talk both before and after they had relieved each other's needs for sexual release. The touching was never rough; it was always soft and tantalizing. It always led to higher and higher level of anticipation and eventual gratification that seemed to top each preceding encounter.

Ruthie was in love again. Not in a way she had ever anticipated but love was love. There was another human being who found her appealing and cared for her. It had been a while and the quality of this tryst was so much more fulfilling than anything she had previously experienced that Ruthie actually began to turn outward and reveal more of herself rather than remain within the confines of her inner psyche. She was enjoying life; she was enjoying Deborah. Life finally delivered on her terms and she was happy!

It was a hot, sticky August morning when Ruthie kicked the sheet off her nude body. She had beads of sweat trickling from her arm pits and from the folds beneath her large breasts. The air in the small room that fronted for a bedroom in the tiny trailer equated to a heavy musk odor that said the preceding night had been another to log as serious sexual involvement. As per usual, Ruthie shimmied off the tossing waterbed, planted her feet to the floor and without bothering to don a stitch of clothes wandered past the curtain that passed as a door for the miniscule bedroom. She was in full anticipation of wrapping her arms about Deborah, hugging her closely and nuzzling her lips against her lover's neck. . . then her breasts. . . and probably more before she could find any excuse to stop long enough to cleanse her mouth with a shot of orange juice.

Unfortunately, Deborah wasn't in the next room, such as it was. Ruthie concluded that she must have stepped out to check the mail at the box a short walk away. She pushed open the door which still caught on each opening due to the hinges being sprung. Standing in the doorway, stark naked, her large, pendulous breasts swaying with each move and her coal black triangle in clear evidence, she looked down the small driveway for a sign that she had been right about Deborah fetching the mail from the outlying box. She wasn't there.

Somewhat perplexed, Ruthie closed the door, mostly, turned to the small icebox and grabbed for the half-full container of pulp-laden orange juice from Florida. Prying open the end of the container she wolfed down a heavy snort of the juice before she noticed a note on the Formica table. It was folded and stand-ing tent-like with only the word "Ruthie" being on the outer side. Ruthie's reading was better now because part of the program at the clinic had been to improve the basic operational skills of the attendees such as with reading, writing and basic math for use at the supermarket and so forth.

It was a note from her lover. She smiled, pulled the chair out and sat her naked butt onto the chilled plastic surface. She began to read: "Ruthie. It's been a ball. I've enjoyed being with you a great deal. However, my old man just got released from prison so I'm going back to him. I'll be able to tell him that during this time I never once had sex with a man. Deb."

A lightning bolt could have crashed through the tin shell of the trailer and pierced directly through Ruthie with no less effect than the slip of paper she held. Tears burst forth like a small explosion from each of her eyes and she screamed a terrifying scream. She was alone again. No one to have and hold, no one to hold her. She was alone.

Chapter 13
Defining the Bottom

The loss of Deborah had had cataclysmic consequences. Ruthie had had close moments with the Radcliffe's and even a few with her father before the drinking got out of hand. She had enjoyed the time with The Dude, regardless of the debauchery and the quartet of simultaneous abusers had even filled a need. However, it was Deborah who had turned the key in Ruthie's lock.

Ruthie hadn't thought of herself as a lesbian and still didn't but the thoughtful comments, the gentle touch, the opportunity to talk about something other than car engines, beer and hooters had been a chance to grow and become her own person. Deborah afforded all these opportunities and brought a sexual appetite to the arena the likes of which Ruthie hadn't seen and could barely deal with. The woman was a sexual banshee and that suited Ruthie just fine. It gave her a chance to put her most spectacular assets to their greatest advantage and reap a sense of satisfaction from the appetite they sated.

That was all gone now. She had had peaks and valleys but with Deborah she had risen to the top and without a word of notice or an explanation that made any sense, Ruthie's world had been turned upside down once again, tumultuously. Only one thing could help to offset this new depth of dissatisfaction. . . Ruthie crumpled Deborah's note then reopened it and tore it into tiny shreds. Without hesitating, she stomped into the bedroom, threw on the minimum of clothes that would avoid arrest for indecency and walked to the front of the trailer park where there was a pay phone.

"Hello?" she paused. "Yes. . . sí. Armando. This is Ruthie." There was a hesitation from the other end of the line and then some chattering. "Sí, Armando. I need a favor and I need it fast. Okay?"

Armando could be heard shouting to the other three morons as he slid between English and Spanish. He was trying to develop a sense of the collective level of horniness of the foursome before committing to making a drive to Muncie to deliver a fix to Ruthie. Neither he nor any of his buddies was going to do it because Ruthie needed it or otherwise out of the goodness of their hearts.

A perfect score of four would have gotten Ruthie her fix for the cost of a night of depraved sex. Larry Flynt from Hustler Magazine would be able to turn this from an episode into a best seller. However, Ruthie didn't get her four vote landslide. She didn't even get the three vote plurality – not so much as an even split. Armando was always good for an evening of lust but without his three amigos he opted to not make the drive. "Sorry bitch. You'll have to get it somewhere else. Later baby." Armando hung up perfunctorily.

Ruthie stood staring at the receiver thinking that it might over turn the vote and get her a happy night, a night of soft thoughts without sharp angles and corners, just a chance to ease her way through the night without the need to think or remember – a night of unconsciousness. It was not to be.

It was already a sticky, muggy day. The sun was bright and blistering high overhead and the din of traffic was beginning to invade the limited ability Ruthie had with which to focus. It seemed that everything and everyone was against her. *Why?* She hadn't hurt anyone. *Why did this have to happen?* The questions lingered as she staggered trance-like back to the rusty trailer. As she walked, her head hung low, twisting back and forth as she walked as if shaking the jug would produce a sweeter wine. Tears were streaming down her puffy cheeks; her ratty hair was in tangles and utter disarray. Remnants of the preceding day's application of makeup tricking down her face in black rivulets. As Ruthie walked haltingly back to the silver and black twenty-footer in the last row, curtains parted slightly to form peak holes to see what new revelation would unfold with the *crazy fat chick.*

The choked emotion manifesting itself from within her suddenly became an eruption of unconstrained loathing and self-pity. The tearful rivulets gave way to cascading tears that bespoke the depth to which Ruthie had been wounded. The occasional sob and sniffle became a wailing that could be heard across Muncie save for the doorstep at the motel where Deborah had joined, figuratively and literally, with her husband. As deep as Ruthie had fallen, Deborah had risen. There is a balance in life, in nature, but Ruthie could not afford the luxury of philosophical meanderings.

There was no lover; there were no drugs to blunt the pain. There was only reality and the fact that Ruthie would have to find a way in which to deal with it.

Back in her trailer, Ruthie spread her arms across the Formica-covered table and sank her head into her arms and continued the soul-venting process of having to let go of a good thing, a thing she had not sought but something to which she had become accustomed and dependent. It had been handed to her in the middle of a lustful, still night at the clinic. Now it had been jerked away unceremoniously in the middle of a lustful, still night at her trailer.

The mid-morning arousal to the tune of the shocking news and grim reality had produced an agonizing shell of a woman. Her thoughts were intermittent between the outbursts of raw emotion that could not be constrained. Nearby neighbors were loathe to interfere and "become involved" as it was the crazy woman in the back trailer and no one wanted to have to deal with her. They were not their "brother's keeper" nor were they their "sister's keeper."

The crying and hair-pulling that lasted for several days was only interrupted with an occasional slug of tequila. Finally, the large-bodied woman, drenched in sweat, her eyes swollen profusely, her hair in complete disarray could not take the agony any longer. She had reached a decision.

Ruthie squatted her large body onto the floor of the small shower stall, its three by three space barely big enough for the woman when sitting on the floor with her knees pulled up to her chest. Using the serrated butcher knife she had brought from the kitchenette her right hand hovered above her left arm, the blade encrusted with stale food did not gleam in the refracted light within the trailer but the blade was sharp enough for a simple job of this type. Ruthie stared at the blade; she stared at her left arm. This intended act of denial was not solving her pain; she had to do more than want to take such action − she had to follow through. She had to slash one wrist and then the other if the pain in her soul was to be abated.

Ruthie's eyes were glassed over from the tears; they were so full of the salty tears that her vision was blurred. Finally, "oh Debbie, how could you do this?" and Ruthie sliced down through the air in an arc that projected itself through the skin and the large artery just beneath the surface. Because of her accelerated heart rate from the crying the blood spurted in waves and drained down through her palm and onto the cotton house dress she wore. Before she lost consciousness, she made the decision to slice the other side as well to ensure that she didn't awake later to the continued heartache. Down sliced the blade through the artery once again, leaving a crust of pizza fragments along the line of skin that had been separated. Now, she rested her head back against the shower stall, dropped both arms into her lap and waited.

It is difficult to tell precisely how much time passed between the last audible outburst and the quietude that ensued. The absence of shrieking noise became as loud as the noise itself had been. Old Mrs. Crunster, three trailers away and the widow of an alcoholic, who had taken his own life, noticed the peculiar lack of noise that had permeated the entire trailer camp. Unlike her do-nothing neighbors, Mrs. Crunster felt some sense of obligation to investigate what had happened, fearing the worst from first hand history.

Mrs. Crunster was well known around the small trailer park. She lived in the two-wide with the brown and white awning; the one with the damaged back end where Mr. Crunster had accidentally ignited their propane tank sending him to *trailer park heaven*. Mrs. Crunster had a knack for checking out everyone's visitors – no one got by her without her recognition as to whom they were visiting. She also liked to be the first to the communal mailbox and see who was getting checks who was getting what bills and otherwise simply being a nosey old bitch. That was the common reading on Mrs. Crunster anyway.

True to form, it was Mrs. Crunster who elected to poke her nose figuratively and literally into the cracked door at Ruthie's trailer. She was aghast at the odor that took her breath away and shocked at the mess she found and that was just from peeking through the crack in the door, well, the crack that she forced wide enough to get her whole head through. The table and the floor were littered with every form of discard imaginable. On the table were the remnants of a pizza that had to be calcifying due to age; the crusts sat alongside Ruthie's "female pleasure device." Seeing this, Mrs. Crunster's head snapped backward as she was horrified at the level of degradation implied by the site. *How someone could be so low*, she thought. Following Mr. Crunster's death, Mrs. Crunster had turned to using squash, the long tapered kind. . . but still, *a "female pleasure device."*

The old lady, actually she looked much older and acted older still, than she actually was. At fifty-seven years old, the grandmother looked to be seventy, if a day, but acted like a person well into her eighties. She poked her head back through the door ignoring the disgusting site on the kitchen table and began to call out, "Ruthie?" She paused a few seconds, "Ruthie?" Finally, hearing no response and knowing that the calamity that had been trumpeted from this location only a short time before and then ended abruptly, made her wonder even more.

The old lady stepped up the step and through the door held only loosely by the second hinge. She leaned her body forward to gander down the short distance between one end and the other of the trailer. By leaning, she extended her view but hadn't further trespassed – such was her logic. Then she saw it. The lower half of one of Ruthie's legs had flopped out of the miniscule shower stall and onto the floor between the bedroom and the kitchen, the two rooms comprising the extent of the trailer. It took a second for recognition and then it sunk in. Mrs. Crunster, shrieked a piercing sound that most likely set car alarms off blocks away as she ran the short distance to the shower stall.

The body of Ruthie was slumped into a corner of the shower, her head hanging forward and her two arms dropped loosely at her sides as they continued to leak blood into a pool that had formed over the stopped-up shower drain. Mrs. Crunster started to bend down to grab hold of Ruthie to help in whatever way might seem to come naturally, but then was so repulsed by the bloody sight that she stepped back from the shower covering her mouth with both hands as her eyes widened to the maximum extent possible.

After what might have seemed to be an eternity but was most likely no more than ten seconds, Mrs. Crunster pivoted and bolted from the small trailer and ran straight away to the pay phone that was bracketed to a light pole over the entrance to the trailer park. She punched in   9-1-1 and shrieked the situation to the operator who tried to calm the agitated woman but to no avail. "We'll have an officer out there shortly, Ma'am," came the only response from the police call desk.

The officer had taken the call seriously and moments later a police cruiser arrived lights flashing and siren trumpeting his arrival. After a follow-up call by the officer and a little quick thinking on his part to stanch the flow of blood, Ruthie was carted off in a white van bound for Ball Memorial Hospital across town. Her vitals were astonishingly weak but the medic on board believed that they could "pull the fat chick through this one," he exclaimed to the driver. "Step on it, when we deliver this I've got a softball game. I'm pitching and need to warm up."

After several days in the hospital, Ruthie was released to Mrs. Przybylinski who had a car waiting to take Ruthie back to the clinic. When they pulled into the parking lot, Ruthie's only comment to Mrs. Przybylinski, to herself, or to no one, just an audible, involuntary response was, "oh no, not again."

Chapter 14
It's Business, Not Personal

Recovery from her self-inflicted suicide attempt was more easily accomplished as an unwilling resident of the clinic than if she had to fend for herself at home. First of all, Ruthie would have doubtless finished what she had started with the crusty butcher knife. Second, it was a drug-free environment so that wouldn't become a crutch and simultaneous burden during recovery. . . and the booze was also out of the question. Her attitude, however, was even worse than before. She had had a conspicuous loss that had been the catalyst to send her to the clinic the first time. However, this time the loss was compounded by the self-inflicted wounds that needed to heal

Mrs. Przybylinski was growing weary of the repeated attempts to cut through the solid outer shield that Ruthie had erected against further incursion and pain.

The days were the same as before - they were consummately boring, filled within a meaningless drill that was intended as a distraction from the soul-wrenching demands made on the body by chemical dependency. The drugs were not so much the issue this time but Ruthie's state of mind was appreciably the same as that of the others who populated the women's dorm.

Some time passed. Ruthie's state of mind continued to linger in a stagnant place incapable of resurrecting itself from the damage inflicted by others and the resulting self-pity. Ruthie knew there were others about her as she shuffled through the process but it was as if she were wearing ear plugs and blinders. She might have been in some sort of transcendental state that precluded her recognition of reality, but to a fair degree that had been her condition since just after birth. She noticed there were some pooled together in hushed conversations; she absently saw others at the meetings, at meals, in the showers, in the dorm before lights-out and occasionally in the fenced green area behind their compound. If ever required by the police to identify any of these individuals they would have to turn to another source as Ruthie's memory banks had not registered any faces, names, or specific recollections since being brought in this time.

The afternoon was unseasonably hot for late-October. The leaves had just begun to turn a week or so earlier and then a sudden surge of unseasonal warmth had blown up the Mississippi and Ohio Valleys and climatically engulfed central Indiana in a heat wave. It was a great time to get outside as much as possible because in the back of everyone's minds was the understanding that the weather could reverse itself overnight and quickly become a serious chill, then flat out cold with snow, sleet, freezing rain and the like. After all, this was Indiana and it had never been confused with an idyllic setting unless, of course, you are a farmer and grow corn or soy beans.

Ruthie's hair had been combed out by a beautician who came in once a week to do a work-over on the female detainees to give them something of an uplift. Her hair had been pulled back into a vertical roll in the back and pinned through with a large clip. In light of the weather, she had donned a scoop necked cotton top and because of her build it turned out to be quite revealing. Despite her pride in this singular source of envy by others, her chest was still doing its magic in her behalf.

A half hour into the outdoor recess from instructions about balancing one's checkbook, a young woman also in her early twenties approached Ruthie and joined her at a picnic table. The young woman, Francine, was the first to actually speak to Ruthie during this visit when she innocently offered, "gee, those things look fabulous, are they real?" as she nodded toward Ruthie's chest.

Ruthie's head turned from nowhere to see what had been said and who was saying it. "Huh," she responded.

"I said, your boobs, are they real cuz they're magnificent." Francine absently folded her arms over her own chest as she spoke, a habit many women have when they are self conscious about being too big or too small.

Ruthie heard the question this time and her first thought was Deborah. Deborah had also held a great attraction to her chest . . . and look how that had ended. She hadn't been able to remedy the pain that that had engendered but she wasn't going to sit here and be seduced into another such relationship which clearly had the potential to end the same way. No good could come of being hooked up with another woman – they could cause too much pain.

Ruthie also folded her arms in a psychologically defensive posture, looked Francine up and down and began to bolt from the picnic bench. "Wait! I wasn't being offensive, honest. And . . . and I wasn't making an advance, honest. I've been told your name is Ruthie and someone told me a little about why you're here, I'm really sorry about all that."

Ruthie, softened her visual assessment of Francine and squeaked out a small smile from the corner of her mouth. "Thanks," said Ruthie. "Life can be a bitch, ya know?"

"Yeah, I know," responded Francine. "How else could you account for any of us being here, right?"

That seemed to strike a chord with Ruthie whose arms removed from guard status and rested on the table. She turned slightly toward Francine. "Why are you here?" she asked.

"I work at a club. . . dancing." Ruthie's eyes widened a little. Francine proceeded, "yeah, I know what you're thinking and no, I just dance. That's it. From time to time I might hook up with a customer but that's my own doing and it's just to knock the edge off, ya know?" The brunette's hair fluttered in the warm breeze as she spoke and even without much makeup, Ruthie could see that Francine was uncommonly pretty. Her bone structure afforded her an appearance that slid between the definitions of gaunt and chiseled. She looked genuine and not contrived. She wasn't phony.

"Ruthie? Right?" asked Francine.

114

"Yeah, I'm Ruthie and what's your name?" she responded as she finished rotating on the picnic bench seat to completely face Francine, hunching over slightly as she leaned on both elbows.

"I'm Francine," she paused then went on. "I dance, like I said down at the SSGC four nights a week and I just thought that maybe with all that you've got hangin' out there, maybe you'd be a good one to dance there also. What do you think?" Francine extended her arm across the table ostensibly offering an apple to Ruthie but bumping into Ruthie's right side protrusion. "Yep. Those are the real deal alright. Wow. What I wouldn't give to have those. I could dance anywhere if I had what you've got." She left the apple in front of Ruthie.

"You didn't tell me why you're in here Francine." Ruthie blushed slightly as her cheeks reddened as a result of the touch and the compliment.

"Well, as I said, I don't turn tricks at the SSGC, I just dance but there is a pretty steady flow of drugs through the place. Some even say that the cops are behind the distribution. Last week, apparently I collapsed on stage and here I am following a check out at the hospital."

Lights were beginning to flash on and off in Ruthie's head despite her minimal analytical skills. She looked down into the deep gorge carved down the center of her chest and at the mountainous orbs that sat astride the rift line. She looked back up toward Francine as she also made the connection to the statement about the free-flow of drugs. *It'd be the best of both*

worlds, she thought, I could do what I was probably always in-
tended to do – share these babies with the world, not just one
person at a time. And I could get what I need to clamp down on
some of my memories: dad, the Radcliffe's, the dude, Bob, the
four slobs from Nap Town, and that bitch Deborah. "You really
think I might have a chance at doing that. . . dancing I mean?"
Ruthie stood at the edge of the table. "Ya see, my boobs are my
greatest asset but may too big for a dancer."

Francine responded with a giggle. "Sure. You know the
saying, different strokes for different folks. Well, there's probably those out there who wouldn't like your butt or legs but
they're going to love those things. Keep in mind; ninety-five
percent of men in this country are 'tit men'."

"Really?" Ruthie asked in stark amazement."

"Well, actually, don't quote me on the percentage, but it
sure seems like it, especially when you're on the small side like
me." Francine paused and swallowed a drink of Dr. Pepper before going on. "Hell, ya know in a lot of clubs you can't show
anything down below so you got to count on your chest for
turnin' the guys on and making those tips.

"You mean you get paid to dance at this place, you make
tips also, and. . . and you can score some dope as well?" Ruthie
seemed perplexed at a situation that seemed to good to be true
and it was being handed to her by a beautiful girl who didn't
seem to want to use her and then dump on her. Francine seemed
genuinely nice. "Where do I sign up?" asked Ruthie.

"Well, we've got to get out of here first. I think I can arrange that. I'll give a call to my boss. You got a place to stay when you're out?" she asked Ruthie.

"Yeah, unless some squatter has moved into my trailer it's down on the Southside along Maple. And tell me again, what is this SSGG place?"

Francine smiled, "it's the SSGC, the South Side Gentlemen's Club. Despite the name, it's a bar. Good owner, good bouncer, plenty of locals come in and we get our share of the college guys – the ones who can't score with the coeds and have no idea what a woman's body looks like. We're kind of their first sex education class, so to speak. When we get out I'll take you down there to meet Freddy. You'll like him, okay?"

The two of them rose as a bell had just sounded to end the recreation period and signal the next installment of how to balance their checkbook. Francine put her arm over the shoulder of Ruthie as they headed for the door – Francine was smiling and for the first time in quite a while Ruthie was smiling – not just on the outside but it began all the way down in the depths of her soul and worked out through a toothy, broad grin.

Chapter 15
The South Side Gentlemen's Club

Muncie, Indiana, had been established as a city at about the time the Civil War ended – no cause and effect intended, just coincidence. It had been a major center for Indians prior to its incorporation and even considered to be the state capital at one time before Indian-No Place won that advantage. In large measure, Ball State University was established at Muncie as a result of the charitable contributions by the five Ball brothers who had established a glass factory in town which, among other products, produced the Ball canning jars. And were logic to prevail, this was all possible because east central Indiana was underlain by a large deposit of natural gas, fundamental to glass works.

After the turn of the century, the nineteenth to the twentieth, or 1905 to be more specific, the more affluent element of the community had sought to create a place where the gentlemen of that era could collect to share stories of their trade and commerce, discuss the latest advances in technology, and key among all topics – politics. Much like the men's clubs in England, the South Side Gentlemen's Club was created with these high principles in mind as the backdrop for a proper drinking establishment.

The fortunes of the SSGC rose and fell with the fortunes of Muncie as with the fortunes of Indiana and the nation over time. It had seen good times; it had seen tough times. Ownership changed hands with increasingly regularity as time moved forward and by the 1960s, the club had become the province of Howard Fink. Howard had been an attorney of the ambulance-chasing variety. His name was all too well known throughout Muncie, usually in sardonic terms.

Howard came by the SSGC by virtue of one of the tactics that one would expect from a man of his caliber. The prior owner had been critically injured in a car accident and Howard, ever present as the ambulance pulled into the emergency wing of the hospital, was immediately bedside with the injured man. Ensuring that his final wishes would be fulfilled and his loved ones taken care of. Howard extracted as part of his fee a signed statement giving him ownership of the club.

Howard Fink had viewed the SSGC as a distraction from his normal practice, such as it was. He hadn't paid a great deal of attention to his club's clientele, the revenue or expenses, or conditions for the licensing of the facility. As time passed, however, this oversight became increasingly evident to the portly man with the bushy mustache and whose shirts daily reflected his luncheon tastes. He remembered the social register as being card-carrying members of the exclusive facility in years past. He had heard of the role that the club played during the depression era and the period of Prohibition. He had seen how the club had changed following WWII. The 1950s had been lean years for the club according to the local press and now the sixties were proving to be a different kettle of fish entirely.

Muncie had changed as well. It had become home to a large number of migrants who had moved north from Kentucky and Tennessee to escape the hard times found in the back hills as the coal mining industry began to slump. Howard decided in the early sixties to reflect the sign of the times and remove the SSGC as a private club and open it to the public. There were simply too few individuals willing to pay a club membership, besides the neighborhood in which the club was located had begun to reflect an inner city blight that would eventually encompass the inner cities of most "rustbelt" communities.

The decision to "go public" had been a fateful decision. It had been the only possible choice if Fink were to continue to operate the club, however, it was like opening Pandora's Box. Immediately, the club moved from a region wide, private social club for *gentlemen of distinction* to a neighborhood bar. The clientele, overnight, morphed form business suits and silk ties to blue jeans and sweatshirts – and those were the more discriminating customers. Down-and-outers, flat-out alcoholics, and derelicts were more commonly the trade serviced by the SSGC. The bar was located just on the south side of downtown so it was quite centrally located and near the haunts for all the transients and vagrants who could muster the price of a bottle of beer.

As the war in Vietnam kicked into high gear, more young men got themselves into college rather than be floating willy-nilly in low paying jobs and remain vulnerable to the draft. The college deferment meant that the enrollment at the local college had more young men in attendance that had been the case previously.

Recognizing the situation with the draft and the ballooning male enrollment at BSU, Fink made another fateful decision for his SSGC: employ Go-Go dancers as a means of salacious entertainment in this Bible Belt town that had no other such entertainment. After greasing a few palms, a crack in the city code was found that enabled the shyster lawyer to put half-naked dancers on stage to help sell his beer and his watered-down mixed drinks.

Fink had found his calling. Not only had changing over from the gentlemen's club to a neighborhood bar meant dramatically increased revenues, the choice to put the dancers before the public had a mushrooming effect.

Fink's manager of the club was a man named Salvatore "the Slugger" Verducci. Legend had it that Salvatore had been a *made man* with the Chicago mob under Sam Gigliotti in the 1950s. He had earned the nickname, as all made men seemed to have, by his prodigious use of a baseball bat, a Louisville Slugger, to make Mr. Gigliotti's point for him. If you didn't pay, Sal would knee cap you with the Slugger. If you in any way threatened Mr. Gigliotti, Sal would crack your skull with the Slugger. If given the specific order to terminate, Sal would use the bat to pulverize the hapless individual into a human form of ground beef. There was an unofficial body count attributed to Sal that had never been officially proved by the police, so good was the effort to cover their tracks and bribe officials through the mob.

When Tony "Big Finger" Apparicio pushed Gigliotti from power in the Chicago syndicate, Sal "the Slugger" tried working solo for a period but to no benefit. Stopping to get gasoline on a drive between Cincinnati and Chicago one day, Sal "the Slugger" took time for a beer at the SSGC – it was the closest bar to the gas station. Fink got to talking to "Slugger" and one thing led to another and Slugger had a job.

For obvious reasons Fink felt comfortable in the club's day-to-day operations resting in the hands of Sal. He knew no one would rip him off with Sal in charge; the biggest threat would be to keep the baseball bat under the bar and not let Sal start splitting heads when the spirit moved him.

Part of the responsibility that Sal wielded as the manager of the SSGC was that he hired the entertainment, whether a local rock band, dancers or even a magician he unthinkingly scheduled during one Christmas season. Sal didn't give two hoots about the music – loud was one of the two qualifications. The other was that it not be country. Sal was a Chicago boy. You play country and western near him and your brain is likely to drain down the front of your face before you know what hit you. He *really* didn't like country music.

The fun part of his job was conducting the auditions for the dancers. The *dancing* business was a crappy job so the turnover rate was appalling. The crowd seemed to like 'em lean; Sal liked 'em "meaty" like his mother had been. The catch was that most were lean. The only accommodation to "meaty" was the overhang that some had from recently having had a baby and that wasn't "pretty fat" – that was disgusting to Sal, and to the customers.

Imagine Sal's surprise and exhilaration when Francine came to work after her stint at the clinic and brought with her this luscious piece of Rubenesque pulchritude who wanted to dance for him. The bar was clear of patrons save for one old timer so drunk he had been in a back booth for two straight days. It was assumed that he was still alive as he wasn't as yet stinking up the place. "Whatcha got there baby?" he said to Francine as he enveloped one of her butt cheeks in his right hand and squeezed gently.

"I found someone I thought you might like, Sal. I went into that stinking clinic for you to find someone like you asked, jeez, I don't want to do that again. Look, Sal, she's not just a dancer but a Slugger Salvatore-type dancer. Ya' happy baby?" She smiled and tugged Ruthie forward to face Sal. "Look at these things, baby, has she got what you like, or what?" Francine slipped backward to allow Sal to focus on Ruthie. It was if he were an animal salivating before a meal.

"Yeah, you done good, baby. Can she dance?"

"That remains to be seen," Francine said, "but even if she can't you can teach her. . . right?"

"Sure," Sal responded, "the guys don't come in here for an Arthur Murray lesson anyway. They come in to see some T&A. And baby, she's got it. Thanks Francie, there's a C-note in this for you. . . give it to you when I'm done with her here."

Sal reached down and took Ruthie's hands as he smiled at her. "Try not to feel uncomfortable sweetie. Sal's here to help you. Sal will be just like your daddy." Sal could feel the electricity that bolted through Ruthie's body as he referred to her daddy. So he decided to close this step with one last thought: "Sal is here for ya', whatever you need – just ask. Now. Let's get started. We need to see if you can dance and we need to talk about your costumes."

Ruthie lit up like the Christmas tree at Rockefeller Plaza – she beamed enthusiasm through every pore at the words, "your costumes."

Chapter 16
The Emperor's Clothes

Ruthie had to undergo several stages of metamorphosis beginning with the fact that she couldn't dance a step. She was so self-conscious about stripping down in front of a room full of howling men that she actually pee'd on the stage floor the first time she had to confront this particular demon. This just didn't feel right, she thought, but since the time with the Radcliffe's she had known that her future was tied to her magnificent bosom. If this opportunity weren't tailor made for her, nothing in life would be, so embarrassment be damned, full speed ahead.

The Slugger had been very thoughtful in seeing to it that several costumes were provided for Ruthie. The truth be known, they couldn't have cost a great deal – after all, only postage stamps and microchips would have been smaller. Ruthie spent hours listening to the blare of amplified guitars and tinny horns, the rumble of drum heads and the nasal belching of various named and unnamed rockers as she watched Francine. As Ruthie thought back to her tryst with Deborah she got all goosepimply when she looked at Francine's body. Still. . . Ruthie didn't see herself as a lesbian but Francine was looking better and better.

Francine was most likely twenty-six or twenty-seven years old. And it was equally obvious that she must have a membership at a gym where she'd work out to keep her legs, butt, and abs as tight as banded steel. In her routine she would where strap-backed heels and a tight little G-string after shedding whatever top she had had on to work her way through the groping hands to get to the stage. When the Muncie city council would begin their periodic purge of all immorality, Francine would adopt a pair of brightly colored pasties and refrain from any vulgar acts for her customers. However, once the periodic purge subsided it would be business as usual and that meant a little crop top the guys could peak under when she was on stage and then its prompt removal to quickly liven things up. Francine's long, flowing obsidian-colored hair cascaded over her shoulders but not so far as to obscure what the guys came to see. She was also delicate with her makeup suggesting that she had had some reasonable tutelage prior to her descent into the world of small town debauchery. Her makeup served to accentuate her naturally beautiful skin and facial features and not create some sort of surrealistic mask. Her dancing was good, but then no one in the bar cared if she could perform Swan Lake or if she just stood in one spot so they could better focus on what they wanted to see. There was, however, a nice rhythmic move to her soulful style of dance as she gyrated about the stage teasing and titillating the sex-hungry crowd just below her feet. Francine had a knack for sliding her hands about her body, up the soft, smooth skin of her thighs until her hands met and then up over her rock-hard abs until they briefly caressed her breasts. It was impossible for the customers to tell if the facial expression, the sighs and the pelvic twitching were part of the act or if she had actually made herself orgasm right there in front of everyone. They didn't know – but she did.

This was a hard act for Ruthie to follow. If considered volumetrically, Ruthie could have had several Francine's inside her; therefore, the abs were not rock hard, the thighs were flabby, and her gut could undulate as readily as her boobs. But there was no shortage of encouragement by the Slugger who seemed to enjoy the act far more than most. The blurry-eyed customers who banged their long-neck beer bottles on the tables to the rhythm of the music through more barbs than tips but the Slugger always saw to it that the tip jar was full following each of her performances. What he couldn't coerce out of the customers by going from table to table, he either took off the tables when the customers headed for the men's room or he dipped into the cash register to even things out. He firmly believed that Ruthie represented the type woman to which the patrons from the south side of Muncie could relate. Francine. . . the Slugger wasn't sure why she hung around. She had too much class and poise for this neighborhood.

A career had been hatched. . . such as it was – Ruthie, the Go-Go Dancer.

After her self-confidence grew and her act improved, the Slugger saw to it that her act was advertised in the local newspaper for Friday and Saturday nights. The more Salvatore Verducci through Ruthie's way, it seemed, the more it was like casting his bread on the water. Frankly, he was more than a little amazed. And the more he succeeded in his approach to attracting crowds to the SSGC, the happier it made Howard Fink, the owner. His ambulance-chasing career had never seen revenues like these. If this continued, he'd have to hire a good out-of-work accountant to "cook the books" for him. It seemed that he was making too much money.

The real surge had come when word spread to the college campus about "the 400 pound Go-Go girl." This was something everyone had to see. Even the heretofore "cloistered" co-eds straight from the farm were part of the crowd that made the Saturday night romp across town to the south side to see Ruthie do her thing.

Ruthie burned enough energy slamming her ass back and forth, grinding her hips in a gyroscopic motion and thrusting her pelvis to the sounds of Jerry Lee Lewis to fuel a small power plant. She worked it. And the more she worked it, the less self conscious she became. Fortunately, for Ruthie, the SSGC had a place where she could shower before hitting the chill of the night air. To say that she sweat is akin to saying that a Mercedes is a nice automobile – both are radical understatements.

Perhaps as much as a year slid by as Ruthie found her niche in life. She was an entertainer, of sorts. Five nights a week she would violate all the qualities associated with femininity and gyrate her bulbous butt to the cheers and bottle-banging of the neighborhood crowd and the college students whose erudite comments nearly brought the Slugger to their attention with his favorite 32-ouncer.

Ruthie would grind and strut, shake and jiggle to the strains of the rock and roll music played sufficiently loud to be heard in outer space. But for Ruthie it was easier to get lost in the moment when the music was loud, nearly ear-splitting. The taunts about her weight were drowned out by James Brown or Jimi Hendrix or possibly the Stones or Chuck Berry, but her favorite above and beyond all else was Tina Turner. She could get her "groove" on when Tina was belting out a song. Ruthie could ignore the crowd. She'd dance, as it were, jiggle and jounce her massive chest to the cheers and shouting of the mamo-centric crowd and ignore everything that went on. At the end of the night she was happy. She'd turned a whole crowd on using those two things God had given her and she was using them to the greatest potential. She'd collect her jar full of tip money and the adulation of a thoroughly turned on Salvatore Verducci. After a short ride back to the same old trailer there was the warmth and fuzzy feeling of her needle with its warmed fluid to pump into her veins. Sometimes she would shoot up before facing the crowd, sometimes after. Before dancing, or after, depended on several variables, none of which Ruthie could name or rationalize. Sal saw to it that she had what she needed but no more – he didn't want any accidents happening to his favorite dancer.

In many respects Ruthie was back where she had started. She still had no one and her self-esteem was pretty much at rock bottom. The crowds that ogled her heaving chest buoyed her spirits when it was happening but once the music ended it was as if it had never happened. Even with the SSGC's crowds, she was again alone, alone and desperate.

Chapter 17
Drugs-1 : Dancing-0

G uys didn't go to the SSGC to watch erotic Go-Go girls – it was a freak show and a good release for those who wanted bizarre entertainment. Most of those involved were quite happy with the way things were turning out. Ruthie was ecstatic at what she perceived to be acceptance and excitement over the pulchritude she thrust about the stage – her devils she dealt with alone at night after work. The Slugger was pleased because her success coincided with his sense of great entertainment and Howard Fink couldn't count his money fast enough it seemed. The only fly in the ointment was the disdain that was creeping over Francine like a fast rising fog. Francine was a class act. Why she still danced at the SSGC was anybody's guess but she had what most men would euphemistically kill for. Yet. . . she had become the *number two* act at the SSGC. She had taken a self-imposed period of isolationism at the drug clinic simply to please the Slugger and Howard to find a down-and-outer who could get up there and dance and help keep the troops entertained. It hadn't occurred to her that some down-

and-outer, especially one with the looks and body of Ruthie would actually succeed and even push her to the back water.

Even though the scales had tipped unexplainably in favor of Ruthie, Francine saw a light through the crack in the door. More and more Ruthie was showing up for work late. With increasing frequency Ruthie would miss a day here and there. Francine's stock was returning beyond its simple par value back to market levels. Ruthie's addiction with the ready-made supply of drugs was catching up to her. The harder she bumped and ground her pelvis to please the crowd, throwing her heaving chest about like a volleyball back and forth across the net, the more depressed she became. The reality of the jeers and cat-calls were making it over the top of The Rolling Stones with increasing frequency and that helped push Ruthie further into an abyss. The formula was simple enough for the back of a cocktail napkin: boo's and jeers = depression = increased use of drugs = deeper depression. What had seemed so sweet was turning rancid.

The Slugger was largely responsible for this turn of events but hadn't been smart enough to understand the formula - it wasn't written on his cocktail napkin. The Slugger probably had an IQ roughly equivalent to the weight of the baseball bat he kept under the bar. Eventually, however, the pieces of the simple puzzle started to fall into place even for the Slugger. He didn't know quite what to do. Ruthie did have a following. If he pulled her out of the lineup to get her back into drug rehab, Mr. Fink would have his ass and that probably meant his job. If he simply cut back on her supply she'd fall into that nether world of half-okay / half-screwed up. She'd need more; she'd most likely go into fits of rage; and most likely she'd become highly demanding and ugly. Who could say what else might develop. And lastly, if he continued to supply her at the current rate he'd probably end up killing her – it was simply a matter of when. He liked Ruthie, truly liked her. He found her massive boobs such a source of arousal that he had difficulty tending bar when she danced. As for the balance of the meat she heaved about the stage. . . well, he thought, it was a package deal.

Given his equally unappealing choices, Salvatore Verducci decided to continue with things as they were. He'd talk to her about her use to see if they could reason a way through the level of abuse that had mounted. He couldn't risk sending her to the clinic and he knew he couldn't turn her off cold turkey.

Ruthie had become the cash cow for the SSGC so Salvatore began talking with Ruthie each day about her life and about her dancing and about her use of drugs in an attempt to get her to dial it down a little. While Salvatore talked, Ruthie danced and reloaded her veins on her way to becoming even more depressed. And while Ruthie continued to use, Mr. Fink continued to count his money and schemed for new ways to twist the environment to make even more.

Chapter 18
Lap Dances & Extracurricular "Sports"

Howard Fink was a reasonably stupid human being but like the camel that can find water in the middle of the desert, Howard had a knack for ferreting out cash. He could find it much like a laser-guided missile found the enemy aircraft. His entire motivational force was directed toward grabbing all that he could hold. . . including stuffing his pockets, inside his shirt, shorts, and shoes. What one can hope to do with a wheelbarrow of cash in Muncie, Indiana, is anyone's guess but Howard was more concerned with the process of grabbing it than spending it. In fact, there's an outside chance he still had the first buck he had made.

Acting on a tip from a friend, a fellow attorney from Indian No Place, Howard elected to spend a few of his ill-gotten greenbacks in the complete expectation that he was actually investing in the *bigger* picture – he saw the trip to Florida he took as venture capital, of sorts. The fellow shyster had taken his family to Florida to Disney's Magic Kingdom. Here, the fellow shyster had discovered that once the wife and kids collapsed in their hotel room following a day of running amok through the theme park, that he could run amok through some of the more curious parts of Orlando where he discovered his own definition of a "magic kingdom." The experience was new to him and he quickly shared his exploits with Howard Fink, shyster lawyer.

Fink had to see for himself what fellow shyster had raved about. He had said that it had been the next best thing to sex without having to take a shower or worry about a police raid. Howard had to see this.

Ambulance-chaser, Howard Fink returned from his tax deductible trip to Orlando with a permanent smile affixed to his face, much like the Cheshire Cat. What he had found in Orlando seemed a better capital-raising concept than torching the SSGC for the insurance money. Now he had to implant the lessons learned into his retinue at the SSGC.

Francine's assessment had been pretty much on target. She did have too much class for the SSGC and despite the apparent swing back to her popularity, with Ruthie missing more and more work, Francine made a key decision: she would not resort to lap dancing once it had been explained and illustrated to her by Mr. Fink. Her assessment was that lap dancing today, would naturally evolve into turning tricks tomorrow and that wasn't who she was. Francine walked out of the South Side Gentlemen's Club and never looked back. Today she is a highlight performer in one of the professional shows on the Vegas strip.

Ruthie, however, was not as circumspect. This was a refinement to the process that had won her so much fame and big bucks through the tip jar (that the Slugger filled each night by skimming from the increased beer sales).

The first week that the new "program" went into effect Ruthie had a chance to *test drive* the process with a couple of the locals. Each was most likely too drunk after the bar had been closed down to appreciate what they were doing. As each in turn settled into a booth near the rear of the bar, Ruthie mounted the first patron for some fat-bouncing gyrations to Janis Joplin while the second inebriate got a more melodic set of undulations timed to slower tunes. It was a test of sort to see which would maximize her performance.

Ruthie grabbed the back of the booth behind the man's head. This put his face deep into the abyss created by the two mountainous orbs hanging pendulously in front of him. She then pulled a knee up onto the booth on each side of the man's legs and began her grinding to the strains of the music. She felt the music; she felt the man. She quickly became lost in the moment between the music and her simulated sex act. At first the stranger sat there and let Ruthie's weight meld his legs into the vinyl of the seat but after a while he was quite aroused and became an active player in the little slice of life that was being played out. Slowly, his hands found her chest. They squeezed and kneaded the mounds of female flesh, roughly at first. Ruthie elbowed the man in the head and the kneading became gentler but she learned a valuable lesson in the process. By the time she had finished the last song she was pretty well spent. For all intents and purposes she had just had sex with the two strangers after working a long shift of grinding her butt around the stage for the bottle bangers' entertainment.

Ruthie had peered into the future and it didn't seem all that bad to her. It was the next logical step in the *development of her professional career. If I pump out a few of these each night, there's going to be some big bucks in it for me, maybe a better trailer. Certainly, some better dope that that street grade crap I've been getting'.* Ruthie's frame of mind improved steadily until she actually appeared to be happy, something not seen around the SSGC since shortly after she started there several years earlier.

Francine's assessment of the role that lap dancing would play at the SSGC was spot on. It quickly led to more intimate involvement. The Slugger didn't have the heart to push the agenda with Ruthie and it hadn't been his idea anyway so he let Mr. Fink broach the subject of his own making. Howard seemed to know the buttons to push. . . buttons like family, love, all in it together, great sex, phenomenal body, everybody loves her, and did I mention, " and did I mention, great body?"

Ruthie fell hook, line, and sinker for the praise and adulation. She saw Mr. Fink as the aloof, highly successful entrepreneur – even though she was not known to have used that word herself. When Howard told her all these wonderful things, pressed a crisp hundred dollar bill into her palm, and slid a packet of dope across the table she all but signed on the proverbial dotted line at that moment. Sensing the slightest remaining hesitation, Howard stood, dipped his head and planted his lips on one of Ruthie's nipples and kissed, sucked, and licked for a moment before righting himself. It wasn't quite what he wanted to do and Salvatore was becoming increasing agitated with the scene as it unfolded but it did have the effect sought by Fink. Ruthie gleefully agreed to serve up the lap dances during her shows and after if need be and then trot up to an upstairs room when called upon. Fink's nipple licking had just created a drug-induced prostitute. All things considered, there wasn't much further that Ruthie could slide. One final step remained before Ruthie would hit rock bottom. . . and Howard Fink would see to it that she took that step, greasing the path for her.

Chapter 19
It Gets Out of Hand

The seasons had rolled over once again; life, such as it was, continued unabated and dreadful for Ruthie. Only television weathermen seemed to differentiate the seasons, Ruthie certainly couldn't. Ask a Hoosier and they'd tell you that that the change of seasons is a weekly occurrence. Four times a year was reality but the weather there is sufficiently volatile that they can be forgiven for their inability to differentiate. A visitor to the area had once commented that he had spent a year in that Indiana. . . one afternoon. And so go the stories.

Ruthie was supine on her waterbed, stark naked, legs spread and lathered in sweat. Her little metal trailer-home seemed like an early version of a microwave oven. Food could actually cook on the counter top and an egg would fry in just moments on the trailer's metal surface.

When Ruthie shook in her waterbed, the waterbed shook and conversely when the waterbed shook, she shook, and so did the entire trailer. Unexplained blips on the monitors at Cal Tech in Pasadena, if properly interpreted, could verify the movements of Ruthie in her waterbed. It would have been a judgment call as to which showed the greater wave action once the bed began to roll – the ripple action of the bed or the resulting tumult that wove across the latitude of Ruthie's fattened frame. One you would expect to see, the other you would pray to never see.

Regardless of the sweltering heat and the unbearable humidity, she lay there moving as little as possible. To move was to exert energy. To exert energy was to wear down quickly and sweat prodigiously. Besides, Ruthie really couldn't move. She was worn out from an eight hour dancing routine at the club and another four hours of bumping and grinding horizontally instead of vertically in the upstairs quarters at the club. The club owner, Howard Fink, overrode the better judgment of Salvatore and exhorted Ruthie to entertain the "upstairs clientele" to levels of debauchery only exceeded by the Tijuana Burro routine.

At first Ruthie thrived on providing the backroom clients with whatever manner of entertainment their sick minds could conjure. But as it turned out, Ruthie discovered even she had a conscience. That thought was foremost on her mind as she lay in a pool of sweat, staring at the ceiling, its imitation wood panels convexed against the curved ceiling were buckling outwards at the corners. The window with its crust of built-up crud from season after season without being cleaned transmitted a limited amount of diffuse light. Ruthie could never be quite certain whether it was early morning, nearing nightfall or something in between given the ambient light level. Her clothes were spread around the room in scattered piles, all soiled and greatly wrinkled. Beer bottles littered the roomscape, the floor beyond the little bedroom, and all horizontal surfaces. A couple vials of pills lay about, their contents askew.

In a few hours Ruthie would have to repeat last night's performance: heaving her contemptuously heavy body about to the jeers, cheers, and laughter of the assembled crowd at the SSGC. Then she would get bounced on the springs of a cheap bed upstairs at the club by a whole entourage of horny college students who were more focused on their beer and the jokes than they were with the woman beneath them.

For now though there was time to think and to reflect on a life lost. The drugs blurred her ability to concentrate on any details, however, the overall picture of disgust flashed across her mind like flashes of lightning in a Midwestern thunderstorm. The pictures were not pretty, they generated a sense of revilement and anger but she felt caught. While she hated herself and what she had become, it was who she was. She had tried to commit suicide for a less injurious episode than this and it failed – it seemed she could do nothing right. The thoughts of exasperation welled within her and tears streamed down her cheeks as if floodgates had been opened. The tears carried the red content of her over-applied makeup and streaks of black mascara.

Ruthie lay in her bed, not openly crying but tearing as if from the soul. She strained to commit to images of happier times but she couldn't find such images in her memory to drag forward. She could find no happy periods, no truly good people, no accomplishments upon which to focus and be able to tell her she was, in fact, a good person, a happy person who was simply going through a tough period. No, only the contrary. All the images were dark. It was as if Lucifer, himself, were sitting on the edge of her bed running a slide projector, scene after scene of how badly people treated her, of her unhappy periods, of opportunities wasted or ignored, and now her darkest period – the nightly debauchery at the club. This image did come clearly into focus. Perhaps it was because it was the latest episode in her life but it also had the most pervasive effect on her, reaching into every cell of her constitution.

The thought of being a "go-go" dancer had at first appealed to Ruthie. She would be with people, in front of people, bringing them entertainment. It wasn't until she began to perform that she realized they were there to see a freak show, they were there to jeer and sling insults so as to impress their friends.

As early as the second night of her tenure at the SSGC, Ruthie realized she could no longer face the taunts and insults about her weight and how that weight affected her ability to dance in the provocative style that Go-Go dancers are paid to perform. She could see it now. The stage at the SSGC was probably twenty feet left to right and eight to ten feet deep back from the audience. It was also raised about three and a half to four feet to give the front row table patrons a great look up at the performer's principle attractions. A brass pole stood in the center of the stage and extended to the ceiling. Many of the girls found intriguing ways to throw themselves onto the pole and slide down, rotating around the pole as they did. Some could suspend themselves upside down and slide to the floor – as further titillation for the patrons.

Ruthie ignored the pole for the most part. Upon walking onto the stage she'd walk up to the pole, put both feet together and holding the pole let her weight swing her around in an arc. That was the extent of her creativity. In no way was she sufficiently strong to be able to hold her weight in a suspended manner as she slid down the pole. She also feared getting stuck on the pole by virtue of sticking due to her profuse sweating. At a minimum she figured that her sweaty body would make a shrieking sound as she slid against the polished brass implement. She ignored the pole. On that second night and every night thereafter, once she'd made her way to the stage and whipped around the pole in a half arc she stepped toward the back of the staged. The entire stage length had a mirror, actually a combination of mirrors, which extended from the stage floor up about eight feet. The room was dimly lit so when Ruthie looked in the mirror she couldn't see any details of the people in the audience. There was just a mass of bodies writhing about in the dark shadowed area behind her. The music was loud, very loud, the tabled area darkened and Ruthie's focus became her own image in the mirror. Ruthie managed to shut out the excessive noise and visual images. She left herself with the image she was there to focus on in the first place. She had come to the SSGC to find a role in her life that pleased her and made her happy. She discovered that as long as she could stand a few feet from the mirror and undulate wildly to the blaring music while she watched her beautiful, massive breasts jiggle, and wiggle, and flop about as she danced she was happy. After all, that was what entertainment was about. . . at least at the South Side Gentlemen's Club. The thought was sufficiently comforting, whether true or not, that the tear flow was stemmed at least for now.

The composite of images that she had embraced as she lay sweating in the bed had not been comforting and had been ugly reminders of who she had become and how deeply she had sunken into an abyss, a chasm so deep she could not see as far as the ledge from which she had fallen.

A common whore. . . I've become nothing more than a common whore, she thought to herself. Amazingly, the only guy that had ever been attracted to Ruthie had been a geeky-looking pimp and drug dealer. And his interest had not been so much in Ruthie as it had been that he really got turned on by her huge chest. All the other guys, who over the past year had been bouncing Ruthie off the bed springs above the SSGC, did so not out of love but for the novelty factor much like the drunken cheers of the other college students standing in line for their go at it.

"Help me. Help me! Help Me!!!" Ruthie shrieked from her bed as she pulled menacingly at her hair, screaming, crying, writhing in soulful pain in her little trailer.

Chapter 20
Shock Therapy

Ruthie was still lying on her bed tossing and twisting as if possessed babbling about something incoherently when Salvatore knocked at the door for the third time. Finally, after listening to the calamity from inside and knowing full well that there was an obvious problem, Salvatore bolted through the door not expecting what to find.

Amidst the occasional demonic shriek and the constant flow from her lips of words at an incredible speed – none of which made any sense – Salvatore concluded that she was speaking in tongues as it said in the bible. Ruthie's eyes had been completely drained of tears, now they simply stared into some meaningless point in space as her head twisted back and forth.

Salvatore had seen Ruthie without her clothes a countless number of times. Because of a certain couple features appended to her body, Salvatore had always been excited at the sight of the overweight woman as she jiggled and bounced in a voluptuous fashion. However, now, seeing her stark naked, writing on the waterbed as if in pain, sweating profusely, makeup smeared all about her tear-soaked face and her hair ratted into knots she didn't hold the same erotic appeal to Salvatore. He now saw Ruthie for what she was in the most practical of terms, a grossly oversized load of blubber, without class, without hope, without a reason to be. Several reactions to such a sight might be predictable at this point in time for someone like Sal finding Ruthie in this condition. He could have become utterly disgusted at the pathetic sight before him. He could have become enraged, not logically but some people are that irrational. He did neither. Instead, Salvatore Verducci wept. Ruthie was his friend and she had always been nice to him and he to her. He had never taken advantage of her nor had he been the one directing traffic to the upstairs "boom-boom" room. He had seen her personal agonies grow with time but felt helpless to solve her problems. . . he couldn't solve his own. Besides, doing so would have been quite a stretch for a mafia enforcer from Chicago.

The problem was here and now, it wasn't a trend line for him to evaluate. She was lying on the bed in excruciating emotional agony as if she were having an out-of-body experience. He had had a conversation over a late-night beer with a customer when the patron had mentioned that he was employed at the state's mental hospital in New Castle, just south of Muncie. Jokingly the fellow had made the comment, "well if you ever need to clear the bugs out of someone's attic, give me a call. We specialize in that sort of treatment." Sal had laughed at the time but realized now with Ruthie in this condition that might be precisely what was called for. And rather than make the judgment himself he decided to call the fellow from the hospital to come check out Ruthie and let him decide what could be done, if anything.

After making the call and hearing a promise by the hospital technician to drive right on up to Muncie, Sal went back into the bedroom where Ruthie was conversing with someone, Satan, most likely Sal thought. This girl had been through hell, why wouldn't it be Satan to whom she spoke at a time like this. Sitting on the bed beside the woman whose arms were flailing about like the rotor on a helicopter, Sal took a warm washcloth and tried to wipe the prevalent perspiration from her face and body and best he could. This only sent Ruthie into a more agitated state so Sal sat back and awaited the professional help.

The man who arrived in a white station wagon with a side-opening door at the rear was named Kent Pletcher. Sal tried not to look at the ponderous boil on Kent's left cheek or the yellowing teeth from nicotine as they spoke. It took all of Sal's concentration to avoid these distractions but he realized that Ruthie was in such an advanced state of emotional breakdown that something had to be done for her and done quickly. It didn't seem that someone's mind could long endure this kind of stress without snapping . . . if it hadn't already – and it appeared that it had.

Kent gave Ruthie a cursory exam by watching her movements and listened to what she was babbling. He used an instrument to look into the inside of Ruthie's right eye, for what,

Sal had no clue. Sal had wrapped Ruthie as best he could in a sheet, soiled as it was, to protect Ruthie from the discerning eyes of another man. It was superficiality at its finest but Sal felt it was the proper thing to do. With the *exam* completed, Kent shrugged and said, "let's get her into the wagon and I'll take her down to the hospital. We'll be better able to make some tests to decide what this is that we're seeing here."

"Okay, sounds fine to me," responded Sal.

"This your wife?" asked Kent.

"No. No, she's not."

"Girlfriend?"

Again, Sal responded, "No. We work together and she has no one. When she didn't show up to work for several days I came to check on her and found her in this condition."

"No problem. You can come down to the hospital any-time in the next couple of days to get her signed in properly since she's in no condition to do it herself and then we'll see what we see." Again the small man with the acne-laden face and mushroom-sized boil shrugged, slapped Sal on the muscular shoulder and began to pick up the bundle that was Ruthie. At once, the small man went down in a pile at the edge of the bed with a singular loud shriek as he had just created a hernia for himself. "I think I'm going to need your help Sal, this woman's a little larger than I realized under the sheet there."

The two men, one small with rubber band arms and the other built like a bulwark with broad shoulders each bearing a tattoo of a victim of his violence knelt on the bed for leverage and tried to raise Ruthie into a position so they could carry her out of the trailer. Together they struggled and could not get any leverage as their hands slid off the sweaty body of the corpulent woman. Finally, they rolled her to the edge of the bed, got her into a sitting position and pulled her to a weak-knee'd standing position with her arms slung over each of their shoulders. It wasn't pretty; it wasn't graceful; and, it wasn't according to pro-scribed medical procedures but they managed eventually to heft the big woman through the door, down the one step at which point they lost the sheet. Now neighbors got the twenty-five cent peep show for which they had been waiting. With a last burst of energy, the two men more or less threw Ruthie onto a gurney and shoved it into the rear of the station wagon. Immediately, the rear of the 1960 Ford sunk as if it had backed off a precipice.

There are good clinicians at mental hospitals and there are bad. . . just as there are good waiters and bad, good auto me-chanics and bad, and so on. Ruthie's gurney was rolled into the rear entrance of the New Castle Mental Health Hospital. The white-gowned attendant who took charge of Ruthie probably fell into the latter category – bad clinician, but then he may well have been a mechanic in his last job.

The hospital was well known for the quality of care pro-vided, the gentility with which they treated their clients, and the high caliber of medical skills attendant at the facility. . . by and large. This was a Tuesday. Tuesday was a weak link in their systems at the NCMHH. A couple of the more skilled doctors were off that day, another called in sick (he was actually in Louisville in a motel with a girlfriend about whom his wife knew nothing). Under such conditions things began to function in a somewhat helter-skelter fashion as the second and third tiers of doctors, internists, and voodoo priests tried to fill the void. Ruthie was about to fall through the cracks in the NCMHH system and into that void. That was the bad news; the good news was that such strife was emblematic of Ruthie's life but she was still here.

To the casual observer it might have appeared that it was the voodoo priest who ran the examination of Ruthie Ross, number R#19720181. The man who was in charge of the evaluation was, in fact, graduated from a medical school; the downside was that most people couldn't pronounce the name of the country from which his degree was granted and that country does still practice voodoo witchcraft. Admittedly, he didn't dance about the table where Ruthie lay, strapped down and sedated however his rush to judgment would have astonished most people. The prescription: electro shock therapy. The hospital would routinely strike a zillion volts of electricity through Ruthie's body – probably not a zillion but only the technicians knew for certain what the voltage was. Conductors were suctioned to various critical areas on Ruthie's body at each of the sessions over the next two weeks including a half dozen scattered around her cranial region. At a pre-arranged signal, the lights were all turned off throughout the hospital and all operating systems were turned down to avoid a system overload and Dr. Suhail Mobit'o, formerly of an African nation that changed names more times than can be remembered, would throw a finger toward an assistant immediately outside the "operating theater." A jolt of electrical current would zap Ruthie like being hit by a speeding car as she stood in a crosswalk. Dr. Mobit'o would stand just a few feet away with a pair of darkened goggles and an eight millimeter movie camera that recorded the event. Dr. Mobit'o recorded his patient's physical reactions to the charge sent through her body. Without knowing exactly what he was looking for, the doctor focused his camera particularly on the cerebellum area for any skin discoloration and any facial tics that might result from the shock. The doctor would quickly motion for the current to be discontinued almost as quickly as he signaled for it to begin so that the charge was less than a second in duration.

Immediately following each treatment, the doctor would hurriedly affix his stethoscope and check to see if his patient had made it through another one of his experiments, seeing that she was still breathing and had a pulse. The doctor's facial muscles would loosen their grip as he sighed. One could almost hear the man utter, "Thank you God for not letting me kill this woman," although it probably wasn't God he was thanking but some bizarre deity unknown to us instead.

Over the two week eternity that Ruthie was retained in a padded environment, strapped down when outside of it and always with an attendant or two by her sides, one could begin to see some metamorphic change occurring to Ruthie through the countenance manifest on her pudgy face. The strain of drugs, drinking and becoming immersed into whoring, which was not a willing activity for her, had begun to dramatically age the young woman. It showed mostly as severe strain on her face. The hospital treatments seemed to have relieved the neural connection between cause and effect and Ruthie seemed more relaxed than she had been for quite some time. Every other day, Sal would drive the thirty miles to visit his friend. At first she didn't recognize him and ranted hysterically at the entry of someone into her space. Gradually, this dissipated and she slowly began to recognize Sal and before her time at the hospital was concluded she had gone full circle back to the type of behavior when the two first met. A new person was born out of the shock therapy. No one was more surprised than Dr. Mobit'o – he'd never had anyone live through this procedure before. *Must be her weight*, he concluded.

Chapter 21
One Last Dance

Recovery from the dramatic treatment imposed by Dr. Mobit'o overjoyed the clinician, would-be scientist whose father had read extensively of the experiments of Dr. Josef Mengele, Hitler's "Angel of Death." When Mobit'o had emigrated to the U.S., the officials at Ellis Island had sought an adequate explanation of a suitcase stuffed full of papers related to Dr. Mengele's research. The name of Mengele had been fresh on the minds of many as the Israeli's had only recently found and transported the Nazi doctor back to Israel from South America for a perfunctory trial and death sentence.

Fortunately, this experiment with prolonged and excessive levels of electric shock applied to the chest cavity and to the brain seemed to have worked a minor miracle. In the parlance of the less-than-humble, wild-eyed Dr. Mobit'o, the results were perfectly predictable and *God* had no hand in his specialized approach to medicine.

Ruthie was a couple weeks past her last treatment and receiving a special diet of electrolytes and high-energy food supplements. She had even lost some weight in the process; perhaps as much as twenty-five pounds over the duration of her stay at the state hospital. When told this seemingly astounding reality, Ruthie's first reaction was to look down and encase her over-sized chest in her hands to see what impact the weight reduction had had to her "meal tickets." Seeing that the "crown jewels" were still intact, she sighed in relief.

"Miss Ross, how are you feeling? You've undergone a major treatment here at the hospital. We weren't sure how it would turn out to tell you the truth," the erudite African-bred doctor explained to Ruthie.

"Kinda tired, doctor. What happened to me and why am I here?" a recumbent Ruthie posed as she grasped at a new and moving target, a new reality in her life to which to adjust.

"Let me see if I can translate this from a medical lexi-con," he paused scratching his chin as he looked wistfully into space. "Yes, that is it, you were really screwed up girl. Between your drinking and a system impacted with drugs and some raging VD manifestations, your system was trying to shut itself down to avoid becoming any further engaged with these outside issues with which it couldn't deal. There, does that give you some idea where your life may have taken a rather bad turn?" he asked.

Ruthie opened her mouth to answer but realized that there was no answer. The doctor hadn't given her an explanation but rather a rebuke. Her lips resealed and her eyes closed emit-ting large tears to run across her puffy cheeks. The doctor con-tinued on for a few minutes until he could see that there was no point in trying to talk with the patient at this time. She'd screwed up and would have to come to terms with it he thought as he gently closed the medical chart that hung from the end of her bed. He raised a hand in a half wave and fluttered out of the room without saying anything further. From his attitude an astute observer might have half expected to find a witch doctor's trappings under his white medical tunic. . . but such days were past. Now Ruthie, thanks to the doctor, had a new companion to join her in the semi-private room: guilt. She would anguish over her sins, poor choices, and apparent stupidity as the days passed before her release.

Every other day Ruthie got a visit from Salvatore, who himself, was guilt ridden about what had happened to her. He hadn't sent her upstairs for the gang-bangs or the private parties at the homes of some rather unsavory individuals, but in hindsight, he thought, he should have done more to head off such actions as directed by Mr. Fink. As he sat in the twenty by twenty room, he sensed great contrast between its stark white walls and the colorful images beyond the window. Outside, the elms and tulip trees that populated the grounds of the hospital fluttered in a gentle breeze and signaled that the first vestiges of spring were blowing across the Midwest. The sun shone brightly but dimmed occasionally as a fluffy cloud slid by quietly overhead. The heartier flowers were breaking through the topsoil and a few challenged the changing weather with blooms – the tulips and the jonquils always seemed to be at the front of the reproduction cycle in this part of the country.

With each passing visit Sal was able to bring Ruthie forward slightly and out of the protective shield that had begun to envelop her as the consequences of the guilt the doctor had instilled in her. Admittedly, it had been her guilt to assume. She was an adult, more or less, and she had to take responsibility for her actions but that logic presumed a level playing field with one's ability to absorb information, fully comprehend the consequences, and make intelligent decisions. Ruthie's injury at birth in that fatal vehicular collision had impaired that ability to make such rational decisions; she did what *seemed* right or what seemed to please those around her. And obviously, such outcomes were not necessarily, in fact seldom, the best for Ruthie. They often represented little more than an extension of the public ridicule she suffered at the hands of others who were offended by her weight problem. So the challenge by Salvatore for her to resume working at the club presented an onerous decision for Ruthie. "Don't worry, baby, there'll be some changes made even if I have to use my Louisville Slugger to make the point," he offered to her as he tried to explain the merits of her returning to work at the club.

"What do you mean Sal," she offered in response.

In his appropriately gruff manner, Sal, with several days growth crawling across his face like the Black Death and deep sunk eyes from his worry about his friend in the hospital explained that there would be no more work upstairs or entertaining outside the club. "If that ambulance chaser gives me any shit over this I'll crack his skull wide open, ya hear?"

Ruthie smiled. That was as affectionate as the muscled and scarred Sal had ever been and it was, in fact, a genuine statement of concern and affection, of sorts. "How's that going to work?" she asked.

"I'll take care of Fink. . . that fink. You just come do what you love to do – and show those big melons of yours around the stage. After all, the club is your home at this point, like me, you don't have anything else. Come on back and dance and don't worry about the hooking and all that shit. It's done. Okay?"

"Okay, Sal. I'll do it. . . as a favor to you if nothing else. You're my friend." Ruthie had made a decision - a clear and rational decision. Was it the best for her? Maybe, maybe not. It had felt good, though. She felt that she hadn't been pushed into anything but had been given an explanation of alternatives and she had made a decision, soundly, as to what would best make her happy and be good for her. This had a clear and distinct sensation that rattled around in her head long after Sal had left to drive back to Muncie. *Maybe this treatment the doctor has been telling me about that seems to have him so jived-up has made some sort of difference in me. Maybe he's done something to help offset the damage that was done when I was a baby. I'll have to ask about that tomorrow when he makes his rounds.*

A week later Ruthie left the state's mental hospital in New Castle buoyed by the explanation that the doctor had been able, by all measureable criteria, to reverse some of the damage that had been done at the accident to her cognitive capabilities.

157

On her hour-long ride from New Castle to Muncie on the Indiana Central Bus Lines, Ruthie formed a plan for her return.

I'll get several new costumes with the government checks that Sal says have started to pile up with my mail. I'll get some flashy things, pretty things that the customers will see. I'll make this a classy act. Maybe I should change my dance style. I can make these babies bounce nicely without all the bumping and grinding. I'll clean up the act. I'll get my hair done and have them show me how to best to wear my makeup. I'll be pretty. I'll be pretty and since I've started, I'll keep working at losing weight – that can't hurt anything. Right? Ruthie fell asleep with her thoughts as her head lolled to the side and rested against the frosty bus window. To those in adjacent seats, it must have appeared that Ruthie had had a nice dream during her brief nap between cities; her face was aglow throughout.

After catching a cab and returning to her trailer, obviously tidied up by a neighbor or by Sal, Ruthie decided to continue with the good fortune and pitched in and straightened and cleaned every nook and cranny of the trailer. She piled up her clothes for the laundromat down the street and checked the telephone directory out on the light pole at the entry to the trailer court for a beautician. She looked for a large beautician ad feeling that the better beauticians would have bigger ads because of their success.

Coming and going over the next few days as she reintegrated herself back into some form of self-supportive lifestyle she spoke to other trailer park inhabitants. . . for the first time in her several years tenure at the facility. She seemed to glow with happiness and she began to get her life back in order and actually in accordance with a self-conceived plan she had developed – activities heretofore alien to her. Such actions and responsibilities had been beyond her range of capability previously. Now, apparently due to the *good* African doctor as she thought of him, she had a life, a real life for the first time. She was like everyone else, pretty much and she loved it.

The new costumes arrived by UPS from Chicago – tough to find in her size, but they arrived nonetheless. And once they did, Ruthie spent the next several mornings down at the club prior to opening time familiarizing her with the feeling of being on the stage once again. It felt good. Sal was back behind the bar shouting words of encouragement as he made his preparations for openings and Mr. Fink was nowhere in sight. . . out of fear. He had brought Sal to the bar because of his reputation and knew what Sal was capable of doing. After Sal's warning, Mr. Fink chose, wisely, not to be the target of a Sal "The Slugger" rampage. Mr. Fink did agree to and proceeded to run a series of nice newspaper advertisements indicating the triumphant return to the stage of the club's premier entertainer. . . with a whole new act. The stage was set, so to speak, for Ruthie's big return engagement.

Friday night, one of the two celebratory nights of the week for clubs like the SSGC, arrived amid a mild level of fanfare Mr. Fink was able to create. And while he wasn't present, strictly out of fear, Sal showed up for the evening's work wearing a white shirt and a TIE. When Ruthie saw Sal on her way to the stage for her first set, it clearly registered with her that her friend was actually more than a friend and that he had put on that shirt and tie out of respect for her and to help make her return that much more special.

Since the time that Ruthie had first started dancing at the club, music had continued through a metamorphosis and the acid rock that prevailed when she had begun had actually changed to disco, probably due to John Travolta and his Saturday Night Fever movie, she thought. The dance steps were now measured to accommodate this new rhythm. And it had the desired effect. She could get her mountainous chest moving to the cheers and screams of the overflow crowd without her whole body flailing about gratuitously. The new costumes helped to focus the eyes where they belonged as well and Sal had seen to it that the lighting had been changed from floor lights to overhead floods so they shone down where she wanted the attention rather than where she didn't.

The opening evening was perfect: Sal's appearance and encouragement, the lighting, the improved music, the costumes, the new dance steps but mostly due to the new level of self-assurance and confidence that had come from the treatments at the hospital. The improvements were reflected by the customers as well. For the most part, it was neighborhood people and other working class guys, many of whom had brought their wives and girlfriends who sat cheering to every move, hand gesture, facial expression, and thrust of Ruthie's biggest assets. Rock the house! Rock the house! Even Sal was singing along to the music. This was Sal, who normally shifts between stoic and nasty. In addition to the town folk who were enjoying the performance were a couple would-be dancers who wanted to check out the situation. Down front, right in front of the stage, were several tables of about twenty college guys – drunk beyond reason from the "get go." Their cheering had a different feel, a different sound, and certainly a wholly different choice of vocabulary to confront the dancer on stage. They were rowdy and obnoxious, mean and unjustifiably rude to Ruthie. Theirs' were not cheers but they were jeers. There were the old comments about the blimp-sized dancer and how grotesque she was. Every comment contained the ill-famed "F" word and how they'd like to see her and the famous Tijuana donkey in action. In short, it got out of control and very quickly. Sal was on the group, singlehandedly, with his well-known Louisville Slugger.

Ruthie gave it everything she had. She tried her best to ignore the scurrilous shouts and vulgar actions that the college students were using to imitate her just feet in front of her spot on the satge. Ruthie tried to avoid involvement in the confrontation thinking about the good news the doctor had provided her and the warm and affectionate comments that Sal continued to offer. She tried to sing along with the music. She didn't want to turn her back on the audience and dance to the mirror like in her pre-hospital performances. She had to face this problem head on and knew that to do so was a reflection of the wellness she had undergone because of Dr. Mobit'o. But try as she might nothing seemed to be working and Sal had too many students to deal with to quiet them all and restore order. Even though the rhythm of the music remained a nice tempo, the beat to which Ruthie danced picked up tempo increasingly, her face showed an extreme amount of pain and anxiety, and instead of cupping her boobs with her hands to draw attention to her assets she dug her fingers into her scalp, clawing at the points of electrode contact. Her eyes were wild and as she began to move about as if possessed. At one point she squeezed her head as if to crush a melon barehanded, she let out a startling scream, dropped to her knees and fell over forward off the stage and on to the front row tables where the students had been agitating for the past half hour.

The SSGC hushed. Students began to back away. Some ran pell mell for the entrance and freedom from the bat-wielding lunatic who was hell bent on settling the score. It would be an hour before paramedics could be summoned to the bar and restore Ruthie's pulse before taking her to the college hospital on the other side of town, past some of the fraternities where many of the agitators resided. The mood had been broken and no amount of disco music would restore the night. In fact, after this incident the club was able to stay open for only a couple months before the absolute lack of patronage closed it forever and returned Mr. Fink to chasing ambulances. Sal lingered about Muncie for a while but had no means of support so his daily visits to the hospital were curtailed and he returned to Chicago where he got back on as an enforcer with the mob. He was shot in a confrontation between rival mob factions a month later and died on the spot.

Chapter 22
Ruthie Gets Religion

Two weeks after the tragic end to her stage act, Ruthie had recovered sufficiently to comprehend the explanations offered to her by the hospital's team of doctors. It had been a stroke and simultaneous heart attack – a very rare combination of events and rarer still to live through. The hospital staff didn't exactly flatter Ruthie when the Indian doctor explained in his attempt at (recognizable) English that if she hadn't had the fortitude of a horse she would never have lived through the ride to the hospital. In some unlikely quirk of nature, it had been Ruthie's weight that had brought her toppling off the stage and it had been her weight, that had fortified her resistance.

Ruthie was retained at the hospital for another week, the middle of which she underwent another procedure – risky, but a calculated risk. Dr. Sapal decided to remove as much of the extraneous body fat as possible to make it easier for Ruthie's heart to pump blood to the muscular structure of her body and propel her with less of an effort being put on the heart to do so. Therefore, once Ruthie seemed sufficiently stabilized and responding to treatment Dr. Sapal performed liposuction on Ruthie's gut,

164

lower abdomen, thighs and upper arms. He sucked out enough fatty material to build another human, or so it seemed as he continued to probe with his instruments.

At this point Ruthie regressed and weakened but fought on as she had through one institutionalization after another. Ruthie was not a pretty woman, refined, or intelligent, but she had resilience and an indomitable will to go on. Her body had been through so many traumas over the past few months that her internal systems began to malfunction. She now regulated her breathing with a portable oxygen tank which the doctor explained should be a temporary condition. She regulated her excretory functions with a host of chemical compounds. Because of the stroke, her hair had turned mostly white almost overnight; there was a twitch to her left eye and her hands would shake uncontrollably from time to time. But she was alive. *I can see now what the Mother Superior had tried to teach me was right that the Lord can intervene in one's life. This was all a sign that my life was heading in the wrong direction and that I needed to break clean. And. . . I guess he had to show me the way the hard way – that was what I brought onto myself. But I'm alive. Thank you.* Ruthie realized as she was driven away from the hospital in a Checker Cab that she had learned a valuable lesson and was being shown that it was her responsibility to teach that lesson to others.

The hack driver took Ruthie to a small apartment complex at the north end of town. There was some low cost housing there and a few units provided by the church where the Mother

Superior had worked before her passing during Ruthie's "The Dude phase." Ruthie was directed at the hospital to the facility by a young deacon from the church as a welcome back to the fold. Ruthie hadn't responded other than to show her gratitude politely. The complex had a mixture of indigents, elderly, some who were simply "dirt" poor, and a few who were less easily classified. None of those at the complex would be found, however, on the social register of Muncie, Indiana.

As a consequence of her treatments at the state's hospital in New Castle, Ruthie's ability to better comprehend what was being said to her, to evaluate the consequences associated with alternative actions, and how to pick the path that was best for her had been greatly improved. She now attempted to study the bible and attended prayer sessions with the others many of whom thought Ruthie to be a senior citizen and with no comprehension that she was still in her late-twenties.

Time at the complex passed slowly on a day-to-day basis but the months rolled by as quickly as money through the hand of a gambler. The days were hot; the days were cold. The days were sunny; the days were gray. There was variation but it didn't seem to matter so much to the inhabitants of the complex. A day was simply a day; they were still on the green side of the grass. Some welcomed another opportunity to look upon life as an experience worth another twenty-four hours and some prayed that it would be the last. Ruthie was in the former group. She had a great deal to live for, to be thankful for and her spirit showed this more progressively each day it seemed. She'd been given another chance. She could have died any number of times in recent years. She had precious little to live for during recent years but here she was, still breathing and still jiggling. The doctors had removed an enormous amount of body fat and cut her weight significantly, by about half when combined with the normal attrition that results from a hospital stay and the nauseating hospital food. She hadn't gained a Jane Fonda figure but she had slimmed to a point of actual attraction and making the experience so much richer was the fact that the bodacious chest remained intact.

As the months passed, Ruthie grew stronger and that strength gave her an ability to move about more freely and develop some tone to at least some of the muscle groups within her. Now she was able to walk to the market and the strip mall, the 7-11 and some of the other princely establishments in the north side neighborhood. The nervous tick seemed to be a continuing condition but the hand trembling that had resulted from the stroke had all but disappeared. She was starting to look and act almost normal again, however, this time around she was functioning with greater cognitive powers than in years past as well as a physique that looked more like that of other women, well, except for the large chest. It still remained the envy of many and the eyed-target of others.

To say that most of Ruthie's friends were gone or certainly not a part of her life would be a misstatement. Sadly, she really never had friends, not friends in the truest sense of the word except for Sal the Slugger. Others had passed through her life using her or abusing her at will and she accepted that as some convoluted sense of friendship since it was all there was to reach for. And as for her fellow inhabitants of the complex, there were some ties, some common interests but no true, absolute, friends with whom to share secrets and dreams. The inhabitants at the complex were a mixed assortment of medical, mental and social ills rolled together because they had nowhere else to go, no one to take care of them, and no money with which to hire it done. Some of those with whom Ruthie tried to strike up a relationship could not understand what she would say, so serious was their lack of mental capacity. Others were terminally ill and were here one day only to be followed the next by a vacant bed at the complex. This was a way station for the bottom rung of society where they might bide their time until it was their time.

It was summer now. By Indiana terms that meant hot, muggy weather with infrequent rain which came in a deluge when it did. The skies could be bright with that pale blue hue that made a person feel good inside; there could be cirrus clouds one day and puffy little pops of billowing white scattered about the next. At the same time, one night would be so still that a person couldn't sleep due to the overpowering sound of a zillion crickets and a serious lack of air circulation. While on another, the temperature might drop so low as to leave a frost on the ground. Perfectly unpredictable. Meteorologists in Indiana most likely don't make much money – the prediction of weather

168

trends might be better served by people wearing feathers and dancing about a fire and shaking a rattle.

Ruthie had a visitor, an unlikely visitor at that. The complex's manager walked the visitor back to Ruthie's spotless unit where he knocked and was greeted cheerfully by Ruthie who was outfitted in a sweat-drenched set of gray workout clothes; Jack LaLane could be heard in the background on the TV demonstrating a new exercise.

"Hi, Mr. Clement. How are you today?" Ruthie asked in high-spirited form.

"I'm just fine Ruthie. I'm glad you are looking so fit today. I've got someone here who wants to talk with you. Okay if he comes in?" asked the manager.

Ruthie could see the Roman collar immediately and recognized the black slacks and short sleeve shirt that held the white-starched collar implant. *A priest? She thought. Come to visit me?*

"Buenos dias, Ruth, como esta?" asked the priest before he caught himself. "Forgive me," he continued, "I apologize. My name is Father Benedicio. I've just recently come to the parish, the parish where you used to live by the way. I was brought up from Del Rio, Texas, because there are now so many Mexicans working in the fields here in Indiana and many don't speak English and don't really understand the American ways. So, the diocese sent for a priest who spoke their language and understood their ways to work with them and give them a better sense of their religion since they don't understand the Latin mass or the English that is used. . . I'm kind of a 'middle man'."

The two sat and talked while Jack LaLane inverted himself on the small TV screen and did pushups from the hand-stand position mumbling something unintelligible all the while he was proving himself to be the quintessential example of fitness.

"You may or may not know, Ruth, that in addition to this facility there is another similar facility, also here on the north side of town that is just for seniors. Most of them have no special infirmities, they've just gotten old and their life has become kind of humdrum. Their friends have died, families have moved away and so on. In short, there's not much excitement in their lives." The priest shifted his weight on the edge of the couch and rested his elbows on his knees, leaned forward to more directly approach Ruthie with the balance of his comments. "One of our parishioners, a repentant man who used to drink a lot but has turned away from the bottle and toward Jesus Christ, approached me with an idea. He's now living in our other facility. . . his wife recently died and he came to me with an idea that might help spark some life at the center."

Ruthie continued her smile as if it were painted across her face and gave the priest all of her attention.

"Johnny . . . well, I guess I don't have to use his last name. We'll just say, Johnny. He came to me this past week and told me about you and explained an idea he had. Hearing of your background I must admit I thought that Johnny had lost the screw that holds his head together but I did some checking and discovered that maybe Johnny wasn't so far off after all. It seems as though you've gone through a lot of tough times and have emerged the better person for it so I've given Johnny's idea some serious thought. Well, here it is. I'd like you to consider coming to the center once a week to teach belly dancing to the ladies in our care."

Ruthie's eyes lit up like Roman Candles. Her face presented a static shot of disbelief. Her lips that had been semipermanently curled at the outer edges into a gregarious smile now drooped into a straight line across her face as disbelief took its toll.

"I know from your expression that this comes as a bit of a shock to you, I apologize. Especially coming from a priest this doesn't sound like anything you'd expect to hear. But let me explain a little further." Father Benedicio shifted on the couch again opening his hands and using them as an aid in his approach to logic with Ruthie. "When Johnny first approached me with this idea I had to cross myself three times in rapid succession to assure myself that this wasn't a manifestation of the devil, but as we talked I quickly came to realize that Johnny was serious and I began to understand the logic in what he was saying. And. . . unlike some other forms of dancing, belly dancing is supposed to be an art form, a cultural representation of a part of the world. It is not intended as a. . . how do I say. . . it's not meant to be a catalyst for sex. It's strictly entertainment and requires some skill. So if you could help teach this to the ladies at the center, it would give them something to get their teeth into, well, those that still have their teeth anyway." Ruthie's eyes bulged even larger as she looked at the priest after that statement and the priest stared back. After a couple seconds of disbelief, the two simultaneously broke into a grin that quickly extended itself into a laugh that seemed to roll through the room.

"Father, I wasn't a belly dancer. It might have been much better for me, in many ways, if I had been, but I wasn't. I really don't know how to do that kind of dance. One of the girls that I worked with put on a little show back in the dressing room one day for a couple of us so I kind of know how it goes, but. . ."

The priest was ready with his response, "I thought you might say that. I brought you a video you can watch through your television and learn the movements. From what I was told you have some rather provocative movements to start with. This will just be a refinement. And keep in mind. . . none of the elderly women you teach are likely to try to hire on at a supper club as the entertainment. This is just a new and entertaining way for these women who will sign up to reinvigorate themselves and have some fun. That's the whole idea here. . . have some fun. I'm thinking you might enjoy it as well." Father Benedicio handed Ruthie a video tape and told her that if she didn't have a machine on which to play the video, he would have one sent over.

After Ruthie reluctantly but finally agreed to undertake the goodwill assignment the priest had left with the instruction that Ruthie should get back to him in a couple weeks once she had a fair sense of how to proceed and he would begin the process of signing up the women for the class.

Two weeks became three weeks which in turn became four by the time that Ruthie felt she could more or less imitate the video. The one thing that worked in her behalf was the same old standby, a pair of boobs which seemed to know how to belly dance quite on their own. Ruthie was now able to sign-on with Father Benedicio, quite cheerfully, and indicate that the three of them were ready to proceed. The priest didn't understand "the three of them" and Ruthie caught herself and made the correction. "I apologize. I mean I'm ready to get started."

Once a week for ten weeks, Ruthie caught the bus outside the complex and traveled the two miles to the center where she changed clothes and gave instruction in belly dancing to the elderly ladies who seemed to get a genuine thrill from the effort. There'd be a one month hiatus and then another ten week session would start up with each new class having more enrollees than the predecessor. It was clear, Ruthie had found something meaningful for her life, something in which she found joy and gratification. She was happier than at any time in her life. All these years, she concluded as thoughts ruminated about in her mind on the bus ride home, she could have been doing this – it was fun and it was helping someone have a good time.

Saturday nights were the big time for the old folks at the center. An afternoon of shuffle board and bingo was followed by the customary meat loaf dinner with mashed potatoes and peas, an oven roll, some Jello and a red-colored drink that the men had taken to referring to as "bug juice," the meaning being lost but probably having an army connotation. With dinner behind them the entertainment would usually launch at about six-thirty or seven in the evening and included some square dancing, a demonstration of the crafts that were handmade during the weekdays, and ended with the belly dancing demonstration. In the beginning it was Ruthie who performed but the idea was and became a demonstration by each of the class participants each week. Ethel who was a widow woman from Converse, Indiana, and had a build not unlike that of Ruthie became the most active devotee of the belly dancing instructions and performances. She would lead the others and get them involved so that Ruthie could sit back and watch her handiwork from the audience. Ethel bonded to Ruthie as if the latter were her own daughter and the belly dancing routine became the glue that held them together like mother and daughter or older and younger sisters. Once again, Ruthie finally had someone who cared.

Chapter 23
And The Music Plays On

One thing that the doctors had not checked for but which continued to live on within Ruthie quietly awaiting its opportunity was a large blood clot. That clot manifest itself during one of Ruthie's instructional periods at the center when she was showing a group of six women how to make a quick transition from a shimmy walk to a belly roll. The clot that resulted from the liposuction had lodged in her right inner thigh and became dislodged during the shimmy walk, a standard part of the traditional belly dance. It traveled upward until moving through the vena cava and lodged in the right ventricle like a stealthy commando operation to take out the enemy command post.

The culmination of a life of pain and suffering came quickly but painfully as Ruthie dropped to the floor on her knees, clutching at her chest and with an expression of terror on her face as she looked at her friend, Ethel. There was barely time for facial recognition before the grimace on her face relaxed, her arms dropped away and Ruthie fell face forward onto the cement floor concussing her head and breaking her nose as well.

Ethel's husband had had an aneurism on his aorta with a similar set of consequences that followed in rapid succession giving rise to Ethel's residence at the center. She knew before she knelt to help her friend that there was no point, life had come and now life had gone. Nonetheless, she knelt beside the brave woman who for thirty years, more or less, had battled adversity at a level that would have crushed most people.

A few days later, following the obligatory autopsy, Father Benedicio eulogized Ruthie as a young woman who had overcome all the trauma that life can throw at a person and emerged to lead a happy and productive life. The priest, who fought back tears, throughout the requiem high mass struggled to keep his Latin intact and get through the service. Like Ethel, he had become quite attached to Ruthie but not for the reason that Ruthie had always felt she had as her source of attraction. Father Benedicio was attracted to the smile that was ever-present on Ruthie's face, the spring in her step as she came to the center, and the happiness she instilled in all those around her. She had a gift, a true gift, but she was late in life to recognize it. Those she did touch would forever remember her for her exuberance and cheerfulness and fun-loving spirit because she now was just that. . . a memory.

Ruthie Ross School of Dance

E thel Lynch had very quickly gravitated to Ruthie Ross. She saw Ruthie as a younger version of herself. Like Ruthie had been, she too had been and was still beyond the national guidelines for the definition of obesity. And like Ruthie she had carried a large share of her weight above the belt line, below the collar and between her shoulders. They had served their purpose: they had attracted a good man and held his interest until his age and his appetites took different paths and his body essentially imploded. Ethel had used her assets in ways not unlike some of the less discriminate techniques Ruthie had employed but she stopped short of public display and vulgarity. Ethel had had the good fortune to not encounter the misfortunes that plagued Ruthie's life from the outside leaving her with limited judgment ability and no means of support other than that which her heaving chest earned for her.

Ethel had reached that age where having large breasts was no longer an asset but was in fact a clear liability. They had been proud and full and demonstrated like magnets for Ethel when she was young but when she got her man, she essentially reeled them in. Now, nearing seventy, she didn't reel them in so much as belt them down. They had passed the pendulous stage to the droop stage – it wasn't a pretty sight so she did all she could to minimize their part in her daily life. Life, however, as a belly dancer presented a wholly different set of considerations. It had become time to roll them out again, prop them up and let them take a peek at the public, more or less. Considering that her belly dancing was done in a Catholic senior center she managed to let them peek out very discriminately so as to not give the poor Father Benedicio apoplexy. Every time, however, that she donned her costume for instruction or to entertain on Saturday nights, her first thought was of Ruthie and watching her try to manhandle the massive display that had to serve a specific purpose as part of the dance but not so much as to be inappropriate for the circumstance. Ethel thought this was much like listening to a world renowned poet reading at a public forum with a sock stuffed in his mouth.

Spurred on by Ethel acting as catalyst, Father Benedicio had a sign made and brought to the center. All the older gentlemen who had sat in such rapt devotion to the gyrations of a belly-dancing Ruthie wanted to take part in the effort and after a couple hours of diligent work managed to erect the sign above the entrance to the center. It read: The Ruthie Ross Center and Dance Studio. All the old folks stood around in the late afternoon sunlight admiring the sign while being touched by its significance. They had formally given Ruthie Ross the first actual recognition of her life now that it had been lost.

They knew somehow as they looked at each other and wrapped an arm around the shoulder of the next person that Ruthie was right there among them, smiling and giggling with her voluminous chest heaving as if on its own accord.

Ethel accepted the mantle of responsibility, in Ruthie's name, to serve as the coordinator for the continued belly dance instruction at the center and thoroughly ingrained it as part of the Saturday night entertainment. And at the suggestion of Ethel's daughter, they extended the program of belly dance classes for the old women at the center to a small dance studio for young girls where they could try belly dancing but the program consisted mainly of tap and ballet. Father Benedicio found funds through an elderly admirer to provide the program. When offered recognition for his contribution the elderly former ambulance-chasing attorney simply said, "no father. Thank you but I'm not the kind of person to whom you lay on the praise. I am simply an old 'boob'."

About the Author

Jerry Leonard lives on the beach in southern California with his wife Pat; the kids are grown, each with highly successful careers, the bills are paid, and it became time to write. Prior to retirement Mr. Leonard worked as a management consultant focused on solving university parking and transportation issues around the country.

Mr. Leonard began writing in 2000 with a novel entitled *Out of the Shadows* which will receive both a prequel and a sequel: *Through the Darkness* and *Into the Light*, respectively. He followed the initial book with *Der Schlüssel: Hitler's Key* before embarking on two very different efforts: *Brenda (A Whimsical Look at a Fallen Star)*, and now *Ruthie (A Life Out of Focus)*.

Much of the past 15 years have been spent developing an encyclopedic effort entitled: *U.S. Army Installations – World War II: A Research Reference* – an 11 volume series, the first of which was released in 2015.

See other efforts at:
www.hollywoodbeachpublishing.com

www.ingramcontent.com/pod-product-compliance
Lightning Source LLC
Chambersburg PA
CBHW051513170626
46811CB00002B/809